To Ellen

Best Wishes

Sue Woodcock

12.9.16

Born in 1949, Sue had an interesting and unusual childhood in the care of her grandmother.

After studying business she joined the police and served in varying roles for 28 years. On retiring she went to agricultural college, and now lives on an isolated small holding in the Yorkshire Dales.

She keeps rare breed sheep, five goats, and various fowl. She has four dogs, Froyle, Fair, Brillo and Tara, three cats and enjoys singing in two choirs, as well as spinning and using the wool from her sheep.

She has also worked in the hospitality industry, on the railway, and as a shepherd.

She regularly writes a diary in the Yorkshire Post.

Also by the same Author

The Cellar Pets
ISBN 1843861941 (Vanguard Press)

The Wyvern Rebellion
ISBN 9781843863298 (Vanguard Press)

Murder at the Brass Cat

Sue Woodcock

Murder at the Brass Cat

Vanguard Press

A CIP catalogue record for this title is
available from the British Library

ISBN 978 184386 550 6

*Vanguard Press is an imprint of
Pegasus Elliot MacKenzie Publishers Ltd.*
www.pegasuspublishers.com

First Published in 2009

**Vanguard Press
Sheraton House Castle Park
Cambridge England**

Printed & Bound in Great Britain

This book is dedicated to Elaine Hayes,
friend, and head housekeeper, at the Golden Lion,
and the rest of the staff at the hotel:
a real friendly place, with a variety of characters

Dramatis Personae

The Staff of the Golden Lion

Owner	Patrick Raistrick
Housekeeping	Elaine
	Brenda Royce
	Debbie
Waiting	Wendy
	Giuseppe
	Kate
Kitchen	Paul
Office	Jill
Bar	Tim White
	John

The Guests

Alana Arbuthnot	(niece of Cecil)	Room 1
Oliver Windle	(legal advisor)	Room 2
Wifred		Room 3
Percy		Room 4
Major Cecil Greywell		Room 5
Julia Arbuthnot	(sister of Cecil)	Room 6
Ted Arbuthnot	(nephew of Cecil)	Room 7
Bill & Charlie Grimsdale		
	(employees of Cecil)	Room 8
Miles Knight	(employee of Cecil)	Room 9
Colin Darbury	(employee of Cecil)	Room 9
Greville Greywell	(brother of Cecil)	Room 10
Ruby Greywell	(Greville's wife)	Room 10
Melanie & Samantha Greywell		
	(nieces)	Room 11
Jim Cordwell	(brother-in-law to Cecil)	Room 12

The Locals

Thomas Atterthwaite
(wife Gracie – deceased) }
Jack Atterthwaite (wife Molly) } Farmers
Jo Atterthwaite }

Archie Babble	Council Worker
Mr Morrissey	Solicitor
Tim Royce	Dentist
Doreen Royce (his wife)	nee Williams
Chris and Lynn	(who keep The Station Guest House)
Coleen	friend of Brenda Royce

The Police

Adrian Graves	Local sergeant
Pc Ord	Local officer
Wpc Tatum Barber	Local officer
Pc Roger Cornwall	Local officer
Moriarty (Mo) Tasker	Local Section Officer (Special)
Pc Harper	Local officer
Pc Williams	Local officer
ACC	Mike

Murder Squad

Detective Superintendent	Saul Catchpole
Detective Inspector	Celia Allenby
Detective Sergeant	Jack Cannon
Detective Sergeant	Mike Mullins
Detective Constable	Julia Pellow
Detective Constable	Gerry Oakes
Detective Constable	Todd

The Catchpole Family

Saul
Diana
Sons – Stephen and Samuel
Daughters – Susan and Sharon
Sister-in-law – Ruth

The Press

Andrews

Chapter One

It was a crisp, cold and bracing morning when Brenda walked down the hill towards the centre of town. As she avoided the ice patches and the slippery cobbles, she saw no one, but did pass two cats. They belonged to the new people who had moved in to the end terrace house, at the bottom of her street. Offcumdens, like many moving into town, but they seemed a nice enough couple, very keen on music, and they helped at the Help the Aged charity shop, and went to church.

It was getting so that locals could no longer afford to buy a place, with so many holiday and second homes. It was a beautiful Dales town, with everything you needed, and it wasn't surprising outsiders wanted to live there. A lot of them did spend money, and helped keep the town afloat. It was a pity so few of them had young children, the schools could do with more children.

She couldn't criticise, and knew it. She was in her mid twenties, and was still single, with no regular boyfriend, and unlikely to have children, not in the foreseeable future. She loved children, and most of her school friends already had them. She had only just got her own little house, only one up one down, but she liked it. It was hers, and she could keep her two cats, and do her own thing. Her mother and stepfather only lived the other side of town, a ten minute walk, and she was always welcomed. She often babysat for her younger siblings.

She walked into the square; it was Tuesday, and already the first market stallholders were beginning to set up. Several of them called a cheerful greeting to her as she walked past. She turned left, past the Spar, and then under the old arch, to the back of the Golden Lion Hotel. The security light came on, and she fished the back-door key out of her anorak pocket, and let herself in. From the number of posh cars in the small car park, there were quite a few residents staying. She switched on the bar lights, and went through the kitchen to the laundry room, where she sighed as she saw piles of bar towels and tablecloths waiting to be washed. She took off her coat, hung it up, sorted and started the washing, before unlocking the side door and going back to the bar.

Waiting for her was the pub cat, Luke, a mature and solid black and white, with definite ideas about his importance to the establishment. She knew better than to make him wait for his breakfast, so she took him down to the cellar and fed him before returning to the main bar. It was still only just seven o'clock in the morning, and the chef had not yet arrived. No doubt her friend Wendy, the head waitress, would soon be down, and things would get underway for breakfasts.

The main bar was a mess; there had obviously been quite a party the night before, a twenty first, from the number of tinsel '21's all over the floor. She ventured into the pool room, and sighed with exasperation. Not only had the party stretched in there, there were crisps, party poppers, and a variety of peanuts all over the floor, and it seemed that the partygoers had been unable to put food down their necks, instead they had thrown it round the room. She considered that by the time they were old enough to eat in a pub, they should have learned where their mouths were, but it wasn't so.

The bar staff always put the stools up, but she noticed that someone had covered the area by the bar in what looked like concrete or cement dust. There was fresh chewing gum on the floor. It was going to be a busy day.

She moved the tables out, collected the polish, and cleared the stray dirty glasses, and had begun to vacuum, when her work-mate Elaine arrived. Together they managed to clear the main bar of dirt, and as Brenda raked out the ash and emptied the ash can in the bin room outside, Elaine made the first cup of coffee.

Wendy was already getting the dining room ready for breakfasts, and the young head chef had arrived. He didn't look very awake, and from the clattering in the kitchen, he had dropped something. The swearing that followed confirmed it. His name was Paul; he hadn't been there long, but he knew his job and was a cheerful and rather considerate man, with a good sense of humour that was usually evident by lunchtime. He was not an early morning person. Brenda liked him, rather a lot, but she was shy, and he seemed to have loads of girlfriends already.

Brenda knew she was no beauty. She had heavy eyebrows that met in the middle, and rather plain features. Her face was broad, and apart from lovely hazel eyes and auburn hair, she never considered that looks were her strong point. Neither was she very academic, she had hated school, possibly because she had been bullied and teased. She knew why, and so did everyone else. She was illegitimate, or had been until her mother had married. She obviously took after her father in her looks, anyway. Her mother was quite pretty.

Brenda was good at sport, very good. She had a large, muscular frame, great fitness, and amazing strength for a woman. She always had Saturdays off to play sport of some sort. She had excellent hand-eye coordination and balance, and when she moved she was graceful, and elegant. She was not unhappy with her life, and was fiercely independent.

Elaine was also her friend, but had been at school with her mother. Elaine was fun, and Brenda owed a lot to her for teaching her how to be a good and efficient housekeeper, and Wendy had taught her to wait on, and even the owner, Patrick, had taught her to work behind the bar. She didn't earn a fortune, but enough to pay her bills and live comfortably, and run a little car. She liked working at the pub, alongside the many members of staff, meeting all sorts of people.

After the bars, the corridor and the toilets had been cleaned, and the brass door plates and handles polished, it was time for the first decent coffee break. Wendy, Elaine and Brenda removed to a table in the pool room and sat down. Wendy was watching for the rest of the residents to come down for breakfast. Along with the debris they had cleared, they had found quite a bit of money on the floor, and Elaine counted it up.

"There's nearly seven pounds here, that's a lot. I think someone must have had a hole in their pocket!"

"Can you put it in the pot? There must be quite a bit in the tips pot by now. A little Christmas bonus for all of us."

"Yes, I counted it the other day, there's over a hundred pounds, now. Wendy, is it true the whole pub is booked for the weekend and next week, by one person?"

"All the rooms are, yes, not the bars, of course, but he wants the dining room as well. I think Patrick has agreed, but is charging him for it. He wants his own menu, that I do know. He sent a list through of what his party are eating, and Paul and Rob were panicking a bit, but I think they have it all under control now. I hope they are nice, but from the sound of it, and what Gill said in the office the other day, it doesn't sound as if they are. He sounds a cantankerous old goat!"

"What room is he in?"

"He has demanded room five. At first he wanted another one, but he came over from York or wherever it is he lives, and changed his mind. He came here before, many years ago, but the rooms have all changed since then. Oh, yes, he wants his sheets and all linen changed daily."

"Oh, does he? I hope Pat is charging him extra. More work! Is that for all the rooms?"

"No, just his. From what Gill was saying, it is some sort of family get together. I'll be back soon, that's room three coming down for breakfast, you know the ones with that little Yorkshire terrier. They have it with them so I'll have to set them up in the bar. Back soon."

The laundry sorted, they went upstairs, and soon they had started cleaning the rooms. They worked quickly, and in a couple of hours, all the rooms were done. Downstairs, they finished ironing the laundry, and after putting their hours in the book, they both headed to the Co-op across the square for some shopping. Leaving there, they went their separate ways. Brenda looked round the market, and then headed home, where her cats were delighted to see her. She had a cup of tea, tidied her tiny house, and then in the early afternoon, she walked down to her mother's place, letting herself in with her key. They chatted for a while, and Brenda mentioned the family booking at the pub.

"There's a man booked in next week, booked the whole place. He's been here before. I wondered if you remember him from when you worked there. Elaine said you might, he is a Major Greywell, from York."

The effect on her mother was quite dramatic. She dropped the mug she was holding, and gasped. Brenda hurriedly got a cloth and cleaned up the spilt tea, refilled the mug, and sat down, handing it to her mother.

"What's the matter, Mum, what have I said?"

"Not you dear, not you. Yes, I remember him, a horrible man, rude, nasty and quite arrogant. At least if it is the same man. He was, at one time, the most hated man in town. He made so many enemies here, some of them still around. He ruined several people and made many lives an absolute misery. Be very careful of him, very careful. Whatever happens, don't be on your own with him, he chased everything in a skirt."

"You too?"

Her mother blushed furiously and got up and went out to the kitchen. Brenda followed, and found her mother desperately trying to hide the tears that had sprung to her eyes.

"Mum, what is it?"

"Yes, me too. I don't want to talk about it. If you have any sense, you will take leave, and be out of the way. I had hoped I would never hear of that monster again. Yes, he tried it on with me, it isn't something I care to remember, so leave it, please."

Her mother's behaviour was so out of character, that she did change the subject, and waited until her two younger half-brothers came in from school. Not long after, her stepfather came in. He was the local dentist, and she thought the world of him. He was funny and had always treated her as his own. She even had his surname; he had adopted her when he had married her mother. Her name had changed to Brenda Royce. She waited until her mother and brothers were in the kitchen, and told her stepfather what had happened. He listened, as he always did, and frowned.

"Yes, all right, leave it with me. I think I might know what this is all about, but don't you fret over it, love, just stay away from the subject, OK?"

"All right, Dad, but I never meant to upset her."

Brenda went home, and got ready to return and work in the bar that evening. It was a busy night, and she forgot all about it.

On the Friday, Patrick came and spoke to her and Debbie, the other cleaner on that day.

"This man, Greywell, is taking all the rooms, and is paying handsomely for it. We need to keep him sweet, so can you take extra care? Not that you don't always, but give him extra coffees and that, and can you make sure they all have the new, thick towels and all the best linen?"

"Sure, what's so special about him?"

"The price he is paying, don't worry, you will get a bit extra."

Brenda and Debbie did take special care, and the rooms were perfect. They double-checked them all. All the rooms had been pulled out during the week and spring cleaned, and they blitzed the residents lounge, known as the Writing Room, next to room five, and Brenda arranged some fresh flowers in room five and the Writing Room. As she checked down the corridors, and put right all the little ornaments that abounded, and polished the furniture, she paused to reflect how lovely the old coaching inn looked. No two rooms were the same, and they took great pride in the cleanliness and smartness of the place.

Brenda had stayed at big hotels, when she had been away on holidays, or sporting fixtures, and they did not have the old-world charm of The Golden Lion, known affectionately by locals as the Brass Cat.

Their extra work meant she didn't leave the pub until gone three on the Friday afternoon, which just gave her time to get home and feed the cats, before changing and driving to Skipton, to meet her friends for an indoor hockey practice at the sports centre. She had both the Saturday and the Sunday off, a long weekend she had once a month. She was playing hockey the next day, up at Kendal, so soon she had put work behind her, and was enjoying her weekend.

Chapter Two

The afternoon milking was finished, the dairy clean and tidy, and Jack Atterthwaite sighed with relief, as he could relax that evening, knowing his brother was doing the milking the next morning. He walked back to the farmhouse and as he got into the warm kitchen, he saw his father sitting in his chair by the Aga.

"Tea's on, lad, all well is it?"

"Aye, they are all fit. Two look as if they are due to come a bulling, I'll check them again in the morning. Their milk is drying up a bit. Jo is in tomorrow, do you fancy going into town this evening for a pint or two?"

"Love to, lad. Is it all right with Molly, does she not want you to stop in?"

"No, WI meeting I think. Some rehearsal for the Christmas show. I'll just feed the pigs, and then I'll bring the car round. Do you good to get out, where do you want to go?"

"Let's go down the Brass Cat. I like it there, no problem with the wheelchair."

Jack arrived at the front of the pub, helped get his father into the chair, wheeled him in through the door and left him there while he parked the car. He worshipped his father, always had done. His father's stroke many years before had left him unable to work on the farm, but Jack and his brother Jo had taken over, with their father to guide them, and although a dairy farm was no longer the gold mine it had been, they were careful and had survived.

He ordered the drinks, and wheeled his father into the pool room where there were several farming friends of theirs. He watched as his father relaxed, and sat thinking how nice it was to see his dad enjoying company. It had taken a long time for them to get on their feet, after losing the old place; he had been no more than a teenager when he had taken over the farm, and his younger brother Jo had given up the chance of university to help. The loss of the farm that had been in the family for generations had killed his mother, and nearly killed his father, who had blamed himself over the whole thing. He had never really found out what had caused it, and his father still, after twenty-five years, couldn't talk about it. Soon a friend of his joined him, and they were chatting about the cricket and next season's fixtures.

He went to the main bar and ordered another drink, and watched as a party of strangers came into the bar and booked into the rooms. An elderly, pompous little man with a thick mane of white hair and watery pale blue eyes began bossing the party around. Jack watched as the man then began to order the staff around, and then turned on him, and said, "You, take my case upstairs for me. Room five. You look strong enough, get off your arse and help someone older than yourself for a change!"

There was no doubt he was talking to Jack, and he could hear Peter, his friend, drawing in breath with anger. Jack decided to humour the old fool.

"Don't know who you think you are talking to, but if you need it carried, yes, I'll take it up for you. Tim, which is room five?"

"Up the stairs, right and at the end of the corridor. I'll do it, just give me a minute."

"No, it's all right, lad. Looks like you have your hands full. We have to humour the old."

The case was heavy and made of hide, and Jack picked it up and took it up and left it inside room five, returning to see the old man berating one of his party. Jack wondered if the old man would have the grace to thank him, and sat down again, and waited. He nodded to Tim, the barman, who said, "Your case has been taken up, this gentleman kindly did it for you. Thanks, Jack, I reckon that earns you a drink."

Tim looked expectantly at the old man, but the hint fell on deaf ears.

"Thank you, whoever you are. You are certainly big enough to do it for me."

Jack, who stood at six foot seven, and weighed in at seventeen stone, nodded, and turned his back on the old man, and supped the pint that Tim put in front of him. The old man berated his party for a while, and then walked towards the stairs with them, as Jack's father wheeled himself through from the pool room. He stopped his chair and stared at them as they moved up the wide staircase. He nearly choked on something, and said, "Tim, lad, who is that old man?"

"A Major Greywell, he's staying here for the week with his family. He'll be down soon, to eat in the dining room. Why, do you know him?"

"Yes, I do. Jack, can we go?"

"Already, Dad, home or somewhere else?"

"Somewhere else, I wouldn't soil my lungs with the same air as that monster. Finish your pint, and get me out of here."

Their hurried exit was delayed, as the old man returned as they were passing the foot of the stairs on the way out. The old man looked at Jack and his father, and gave a rather nasty smile, and said, "Well, well! Thomas Atterthwaite, I'll be damned! I thought you would have been dead long ago. Not still farming are you? Oh, of course you had no farm to go to, did you? Still trying to borrow money? Got your fingers burned, didn't you?"

With a cruel laugh, he walked past them, towards the dining room. Thomas Atterthwaite spluttered, and tried desperately to pull himself out of his chair, and almost fell over. He soon found his tongue, and shouted after the little man, "You evil little scrote, you cheating evil crook! Come back and say that again. If I could, I'd throttle the very life out of you."

Major Greywell turned and looked at him, with a sly grin.

"Still railing about that old thing? I hope you learned to read small print; oh, I forgot, reading isn't your strong point, is it?"

"I warn you, Greywell, get out of here, if you want to stay in one piece! I'm not the only one to want you dead, you nasty bit of shit! Keep out of my way, that's for certain. Come back to cheat more of us have you?"

"Don't threaten me, you pathetic cripple. You lost before. You are not of any importance to me, not worth bothering with."

"That's what you think. Jack, get me out of here, now, please."

Jack had never seen his father so angry, and took him out to the car and drove him home. Molly was still out, but Jo was watching the television in the sitting room. They helped their father onto his chair, and calmed him down.

"Who is he? Dad, calm down, what did he do to you?"

"I suppose I'd better tell you both all about it. I've always been so ashamed. It was my fault, in a way. I let you all down; your mother broke her heart over it, as you know. I was too trusting, too keen to get things done in a hurry. I wanted to expand. Interest rates were very high then. I wanted a new barn, and a modern milking parlour, not to mention lots of other things. I had just built the new piggery, and the lambing shed, I needed a new tractor, I didn't want to wait, but I couldn't afford it, the repayments the bank wanted, anyway. Cecil Greywell lived over in Austwick then, he was a rich man. He was into everything, and we got friendly. He oozed charm, and was really pally. I knew he was some sort of financial consultant, and one day, over a pint, he suggested he look into raising the finance for me. I thought no harm could come of it, and agreed."

"You trusted him?"

"Yes, I did. He was helping several farmers. I knew that Wally Peterson had used him, and Clive Sharples over at Ingleton. He arranged a loan, good repayment rates, with a delay to the first payment. It was a lot of money. I thought it was with some building society. I was in such a rush, I never read it properly. I thought I didn't need to get it checked out by a solicitor, and I signed the agreement. You both knows that I'm no great reader, and he told me that it was a standard agreement. I believed him. They wanted a building firm of their choice to do the work, and they were reasonable, and things got started. The new tractor was the first thing, then they began on the barn. It was all going so well. Then the builders didn't turn up for about a month. I tried to chase them, but it was lambing time, and when I did get round to it, proper like, I was told the builders had gone bust, and done a bunk. I still wasn't suspicious. I went to see Greywell, and told him, and asked for his advice. He seemed most concerned, and said that I needed another loan to bridge me over, so I took it, signed the papers, and soon another firm came and took over. They were cowboys, and I knew it.

"I kept all this from your mother, but she knew I was worried, she always did. I also knew she couldn't stand Cecil, but I wasn't sure why. The second firm didn't last long, and again, Cecil suggested another loan to get the barn finished. I began to smell a rat, and went off to see old Jones, the solicitor here then. I though I would have some redress against the builders. I took all the paperwork, and left it with him. He called me in two days later, and told me the bad news. He also told me that the so-called solicitor Cecil had used was nothing of the sort, and he had been unable to track him down."

"Go on, Dad, are you saying it was all a scam?"

"It was more than that. If I couldn't pay the repayments, then I had signed over the whole farm to Greywell, lock, stock and barrel. Their interest rate was astronomical, and the penalty clauses were worse. It said the work had to be done within six months, then I started to make the payments. It was five and a half months on by this time, and I had no money to pay someone else. I went to see Cecil, and he was a different man. He told me that he wasn't a charitable institution, and he would foreclose on me if I couldn't keep to the agreements. He sat and laughed at me, and then suggested that I sign the farm over to him; he would pay me a small amount to balance it up, and he wouldn't listen. I tried to reason with him, but he just sat and enjoyed it. I was a proud man then, so I went to the banks, anyone who I could raise money from, but it was just too much. I went to see Wally and Clive, and they looked at their agreements, and they were all the same. There were several others as well. We got a good solicitor on to it, but we had all signed these contracts, and all of us, but one, Barry Whitehouse, lost our farms. Barry's wife had money, and managed to help out, but they had to downsize."

"Couldn't the police help, did you involve them?"

"Yes, Jo, we told them, but they decided in the end, that it was a civil matter. They were involved, Wally threatened to kill Cecil, and he complained, and Wally got taken to court over it. The lot of us even discussed murdering him, but it wouldn't have helped us, as a lot of our money had already been pushed on to his son and nephew. He took everything, boys, everything he could. All I was left with was the herd, the stock, the milk quota, and a few old tractors and stuff like that. I couldn't even have a farm sale. I was desperate, and had already been served with notice to quit; that was done legal, believe it. All of us were in the same jam. Wally topped himself just before he was due to get out. Clive became a butcher, with his cousin, and moved into a council house. One chap, over in Wensleydale had a nervous breakdown, another was killed in a car crash, probably deliberate, it was never proved. Greywell even got the insurance money from his widow, for that. I was lucky. The Professor on the big estate here heard about it, and offered me this. As you remember, it wasn't much, but enough, and you lads have built it up."

"So what happened to all the farms, did he farm them?"

"No, Jack, he never was a farmer, he sold them, for a vast amount of money. He tried to get the milk quota from me, but he couldn't."

"Why don't we know about all this, there must have been talk?"

"Not a lot, none of us wanted to be the object of ridicule. Then there was a bit of a scandal, and Greywell moved away, probably to do the same thing somewhere else."

"What was the scandal?"

"He was accused of rape, one of the chambermaids at the Brass Cat. Don't know the circumstances, it never got to court, but I think he paid the woman off. The cheek of his coming back to stay there, of all places!"

"Was it just farmers he targeted?"

"No, he broke all sorts. He is a crook, and took so many people out. Most moved away, but there is a few of us left. The worst thing was when I had to tell Gracie what I had done. It was the hardest thing I had to do, and bless her, she forgave me, but she was ill from that moment on. She stuck by me, and started again here, but something inside her started to die that day. As you know she developed cancer about then, and it killed her."

"I remember you nursing her, and looking after us, and there was no money for anything. I think you and Jack worked twenty hours a day. That's why you have never let us borrow a penny from anyone."

"Not quite, Jo, but you were both wonderful, I couldn't have asked for better sons. Not once did you ask for things we couldn't afford. I do appreciate the sacrifices you both made. So did your mother."

Thomas Atterthwaite broke down and cried unashamedly. His sons fetched him a drink, and when Molly came in from her meeting, the old man was already asleep in his chair by the fire. Jo and Jack went out to the barn, and talked for some time.

The next morning Thomas went to the safe, and produced copies of all the documentation, and said, "There it is, lads, you keep it safe. I am so sorry, I have never been able to make it up to you. Leave it be, lads, it was down to me, and raking it up again will only cause more evil."

Jack didn't bother his father any more about the issue, but after milking the next evening he went back to the Golden Lion, where he met a lot of his friends, and they discussed what they knew. Amongst his friends was his old school chum, who was now a sergeant in the local police force, Adrian Graves.

Adrian was strict but fair, and he said, "Before we go any further, lads, please don't plot anything illegal, you know I cannot approve that, but I will tell you what I know, not through my job, but what I remember from the time, what my parents told me. You remember my dad was the inspector here then? Yes, well this man Greywell managed to get him out of the job, over the whole thing. My dad had to take early retirement. Yes, there was an allegation of rape, I don't know the details, but it happened here at the pub, with one of the chambermaids. I believe there was a child as a result, but the allegation was dropped, after a while. I do know that the owner of the pub then, an old chap called Bertram, was either good friends of Greywell, or in his power in some way. My dad believed that, and Bertram put pressure on the woman. I think she was bought off. He tried to find out, and found out something, but a complaint was made, and he was set up. Bertram alleged that he would stay on late in the pub, when he was supposed to be on duty, and would expect free drinks and backhanders over the lock ins, and this man Greywell and some of his lackeys backed him up."

"I thought your dad was teetotal, a strong Methodist, if I remember?"

"He was, and still is. It was a set up, and I think everyone knew it, but the Chief Constable then, who was also a crony of Greywell, didn't believe it, and made him resign. Tell you what, I'll ask him. He retired up to Kirkby Lonsdale a few years ago. He never got over it, the shame almost killed him. Meanwhile, I'll make some discreet enquiries. I'll also tell Patrick what the score is, he might be a bit mystified about what is going on. Why this man has chosen to return here after all these years is a mystery to me. It is almost like he is rubbing our collective noses in the whole thing. Let's meet at the Royal Oak tomorrow, is lunchtime all right?"

After the others had gone, Adrian spoke at length to Patrick. Having done that he went down to the nearby police station and made a number of enquiries. He returned to the pub, and asked if Major Greywell could grant him a few minutes. Greywell's son, a thickset, ginger haired man, short, but rather timid, came downstairs and asked him what he wanted to see his father about.

"I rather hoped to discuss that in private with him, I wanted to warn him about something, for his own safety."

"All right, come on up, he is in the Writing Room. He is preparing for a family meeting about his will."

Adrian found the old man sitting in the easy chair, smoking a cigar. He looked at Adrian and said, "I don't normally see junior ranks, but I expect you are the senior officer in this one-horse town. What do you want to say, be quick?"

"I want to warn you that you have been recognised by a lot of locals who have no love for you, and already word is round that you are back. One way or another you hurt a lot of people round here, and because of you, a lot of lives were ruined. I'm not accusing you of anything untoward, but I think you should be careful. Don't go out alone, and as soon as you have finished your business, whatever it is, leave, because I cannot guarantee your safety, or that of your family. You wouldn't care to explain what you are doing here, I suppose?"

"Not really, but I will. I have fond memories of this place, and I am calling in the family. This is a suitable meeting point, and I want to check something here out. Unfinished business, you might say. On my previous visit, I may well have upset several, but it was their own stupidity and greed that was their downfall. I cannot imagine why I should want to go out alone. I have people to get things for me. I expect to be safe here, or you will be in neglect of your duty. You remind me of the incompetent idiot of an inspector that told me something similar years ago. I thank you for your warning, young man, but any mishap that befalls me will be because you have failed in your duty. It's a free country, I should be able to go about my lawful business without fear."

"I quite agree with you, you should. If there is any more trouble, then I will consider that your very presence here, is not only unwise, and provocative, but is also likely to cause a Breach of the Peace. Be warned, Major, I doubt you are as safe as you think you are. That is all I have to say, good day."

Adrian turned smartly and strode back down the corridor, with the son scurrying behind him. At the top of the stairs, the son said, "Is he really in danger?"

"I think so, you too. I suggest you get him to leave. He is not welcome in this one-horse town at all. I'll do my job, but he will get no favours from anyone, me especially. Tell me, Mr Greywell, do you know what he did back then?"

"Not really. He has always been a sharp businessman, and never let me do anything much. He rules everything with a rod of iron; I mainly do as I am told. Recently he told me that I am not up to following him, that he intends the business to go to my cousin, Wilfred. I think that is what this meeting might be about. He said not long ago that I deserved nothing, that he is changing his will so I never get my hands on the money. I had displeased him when I told him I wished to marry."

"Do you want to tell me about it? I'm Adrian, what is your full name?"

"Percival, but my friends call me Percy. He might find out and see it as a betrayal, but yes, you see, I'm scared, of him and what is going to happen. Could we meet sometime, somewhere else?"

"Yes, here is my mobile number, I'll meet you anywhere in town. You seem a decent chap to me, maybe you might like to know what went on all those years ago. I'll wait on your call."

Adrian rang his father that afternoon, and wrote down everything his father could remember. The story that was revealed was far more detailed than he had imagined.

In the corridor at the Golden Lion, Wilfred watched his cousin Percy talking to the policeman. He had hidden round the corner and had heard the conversation. When Percy went downstairs to the bar, Wilfred found his uncle, and told him some of what had been said.

"Not surprising, my weak minded son was always willing to betray me. You think this is news to me? You have always been prepared to spy and sneak about him. You are the stronger of the two, but I am aware that your apparent loyalty is merely a way for you to sneak into my affections, in the hopes of getting more money out of me. I know you, Wilfred, very well. It won't help you much. I have no intention of leaving either of you much. I paid for your training, and educations, you will have to make your own way in the world when I go, which won't be for a while yet. I'm calling you all together, so you can plan ahead."

"Who are you going to leave it all to, then?"

"That is for me to know, and you to find out. You cannot sponge off me for the rest of my life. Unless, in the next few days, you can come up with some magnificent idea that captures my imagination, I might just fund it for you, if it is good enough. Same goes for your mother, Percy and the rest of the family. Your brother is the best of the lot of you. He told me to go to hell, ages ago. He refused to come to my place, when I planned this, but reluctantly agreed to hear me out on neutral territory, which is why I picked here. Now, go and get me some tea."

As Percy walked past a little later, his father called him into the Writing Room.

"I'll thank you not to chat to strangers about our family affairs, Percy. I'll tell you what I told Wilfred. You have a couple of days to come up with a good reason why I should leave you a brass sou. I despise you. The only decent one among you is your cousin, Ted. He should be arriving any time now. I'm of a mind to leave him the lot, for having enough backbone to defy me."

"Dad, when have I ever defied you? I always did as you asked. Helped you when you asked for it. I've been very loyal, is that worth nothing to you?"

Greywell gave a snort of derision. "I'd rather have someone who is his own man. You are weak, Percy, weak. You are not very bright, and cannot make a decision to save your life. Hardly a real man. Look at that ridiculous feminist woman you want to make your wife! For God's sake, be a man for once! If she and you marry, then you can consider yourself cut off, without a penny. She has more guts, and probably more balls than you will ever have."

"You mean she would stand up to you, tell you just how controlling and unpleasant you are, and you can't take that from anyone, let alone a woman! You killed Mother with your bullying, I know that. She was terrified of you, we all were. She told me once that you only married her to get her money. She hated you, you made her life hell!"

"Yes, you always were a mummy's boy. She was insipid, but she did have her uses. I would never allow her to rule me, no man worth their salt would."

"I hate you, you mean old man! If I had the guts I'd make you suffer, the way you have made us suffer. You're right, I may be weak, but I could survive without you. In fact I'd like to kill you, but you're not worth the hassle."

"Join the queue, boy! At least you've more guts than I thought, and have told me how you really feel. Expect nothing from me."

"I gave that up ages ago. You're not worth going to prison for, but I hope someone does!"

Wilfred listened with interest to this exchange, and unknown to him, so did three other members of the party. In the next room was the secretary, Miles Knight, and the junior accountant, Colin Darbury. They were sharing the twin room, and had kept a low profile. They were both terrified of Greywell, and as soon as they could, they went down to the car park and talked about the situation.

The other listener had been Wilfred's mother, Greywell's widowed sister, Julia Arbuthnot. She was an insipid, mousy little woman, artistic and sensitive. She was also much more intelligent than she chose to show to anyone, her brother included. Having been widowed young, with two small boys and a baby girl, her brother had offered her a home. She had a war widow's pension of her own, but since her sister-in-law's death, she had been a housekeeper and substitute mother for his family.

In the car park, Paul the chef was tidying the box room, and overheard Miles and Colin discussing the matter. By the time he had finished they had gone up to their rooms again. Paul was bright, and thought their conversation unusual, but he was busy, and put it to the back of his mind. He had no love for Greywell either. He and Rob had taken great pains over the evening meal the night before, and had done exactly what had been asked for, but Greywell had complained about almost everything. He'd reassured Wendy and Kate, the waitresses, when Greywell had shouted at them and been unpleasant about the service. This evening's meal would have nothing in it for complaint, he would ensure that. His meeting with Greywell the previous evening left him the impression they had met before, but he was sure he would have remembered it. There was something familiar about the man, and it was nagging at Paul.

Chapter Three

Alana Arbuthnot was grateful that her room was as far from her uncle as possible. She was in room one, at the back of the pub, and overlooked the car park. She could get out down the back stairs by the kitchen. She would meet Miles in the railway station car park, well out of sight of any of her family. She was an elegant, graceful woman, with her own business, designing and manufacturing sports clothes. She was every bit as clever as her mother and on leaving university had had as little to do with her uncle as she could. She had reluctantly agreed to borrow money from him to set up the business but had paid it back almost immediately. She adored her brother Ted but loathed Wilfred. He was several years her junior and was quite unlike both Ted and herself. He was thick set and heavy, with a mane of red hair, and looked more like her cousin, Percy, than either of them. The only reason she had agreed to come to Settle, was to support her mother. She wanted nothing from her family, and it was only to keep in touch with Miles that she was around them. When the boys had been young she had been away at boarding school.

She was dreading this meeting, and knew it would either end in a dreadful row, or her uncle would lord it over the lot of them, and sit like a predatory cat, toying with the emotions of his so called nearest and dearest. She had no intention of ever being alone with her uncle; she had learned that at quite an early age, when he had started touching her up, not long after her fourteenth birthday. She had begged her mother to send her away to school, and ensured that she was elsewhere during the holidays. Although her mother had never asked why, she had managed, somehow, to pay the fees. If she ever broached the subject of her uncle's predatory sexual fumblings, her mother would refuse to discuss it. She did wonder how safe her mother was in the house, especially when she saw the stout bolts on her mother's bedroom door.

Now she was financially independent, she was able to help her mother out from time to time. Once Ted had qualified as a vet, he also gave his mother an allowance, but their mother had sworn them to secrecy about it. Wilfred had never offered anything, and if he had any money to spare, he spent it on his own wants. Alana knew he had a string of lady friends, who were, presumably, impressed with his Ferrari and slick clothes. Alana also suspected he had a drug habit, but disliked him so much, she never investigated it. Percy had, she knew, a resolute and strong fiancée, much despised by her uncle, and she had met her, and liked her. That they were living together, on the odd occasion when her uncle allowed him out of his sight, she knew. The row when his father had found out, had been horrendous.

Nothing like that was ever discussed at her uncle's home, because somehow, he always seemed to know what had been said. She suspected all the rooms were bugged. He manipulated everyone, and controlled them. His apparent bouts of great generosity were always a double-edged sword; there was a catch with everything he did. That her uncle had a hold over most of his employees, as well as his family, was obvious. She intended to find out what that hold was over Miles, during this coming week. She loved Miles very much and they had secretly planned their lives once Miles could leave.

In room two was Oliver Windle, her uncle's long-standing legal advisor, and alleged friend. He was silent, servile and rather serpent-like, in her opinion. She could not trust him, and would speak to him as little as possible. He spoke in whispers, and was a large, greasy looking man, with an oily, olive complexion, and bad teeth. He never seemed to wash, and had a faintly sour aroma about him, often augmented with the smell of whiskey.

In room three, further down the corridor, was Wilfred, and then in room four, was Percy. Room six contained her mother, and room seven was reserved for Ted. Opposite him, in the other twin room was the chauffeur Bill and his sidekick, Charlie, whose exact purpose she never had understood, but it seemed to be bodyguard and general factotum, and all round vile sneak and spy.

Room ten had been reserved for her other uncle, Greville. He hadn't arrived yet, and he was as obnoxious in his own way as Cecil. He was a jeweller but had run into trouble with the law on several occasions. Miles suspected that he was a 'fence' for the criminal underworld and she agreed with him. He was horribly hail fellow well met and loud and crude and rude. He was also an obvious alcoholic, as was his thin and dour-faced wife, who dressed loud and laughed louder. Her name was Ruby, and she was always covered in gold and rubies and had as much taste as a tortoise who had been through a glue pot and wandered into a tinsel box. Room eleven was reserved for their two girls, both as common as muck, Melanie, who Alana was convinced was a high class whore and Samantha who had married a burglar, divorced him, and was now on her own living in Tower Hamlets on benefits. How Miles had discovered that Sam had several convictions for shoplifting she didn't know, but she was aware that her uncle knew everything about them. He apparently found the whole family tolerable.

Room twelve was reserved for Cecil's dead wife's brother, who was an ex-army armourer. Known to all as Jim, he was a keep fit fanatic, and she rather liked him. He called a spade a spade, and could be good company. She did suspect he was a mercenary, because he seemed to have been all over the world, including after he had left the army. If he had ever been married she didn't know of it, and he always treated any woman like bone china. He kept his own counsel about his feelings for the family, and Alana thought, but without any real proof, that he despised both Cecil and Greville. There was something strong and comforting about Jim, he was stolid. She felt safe around him, but as he visited so seldom, she didn't know him well enough.

She was on her way out of the pub, and walking down past the police station, and heading into Station Road, when she realised her shoelace was undone. She stopped by the printers, below what advertised itself as the Old Court House that was advertising the Operatic Company concert, to tie it up, when she saw Oliver Windle turn the corner, and look down the road for her. She likened him to Uriah Heep, and it was obvious he was following her. To turn back would make it clear she was hiding something, so she carried on, and walked to the railway station. There were a lot of people there, especially for a Sunday, and the crowd on the platform gave her a chance to hide herself, in the Ladies waiting room. There was a queue for the two toilets, and she saw Windle walk past the window, and then into the very crowded main waiting room. The reason for the crowds was soon obvious, as a steam train pulled into the station. She slunk out of the waiting room, masked by groups of steam train enthusiasts, and kept close to the hedge. She could see Windle go up onto the footbridge. He was obviously looking for her, so she had to turn left, under a bridge, and round the corner she turned right, and after a while, came to a big and rather posh supermarket. She went inside. She managed to text Miles, and wandered round the store, and bought several items. Miles turned up about fifteen minutes later, and they talked briefly, before she retraced her steps with her shopping, and Miles left a bit later and went in the opposite direction.

As she passed the station entrance, she met Windle, and decided to be friendly to him. She said, "Thank God there is a supermarket open, I managed to get some more tissues, and some cleanser. I forgot to pack mine. Did you see the steam train?"

He whispered, "I did. Why do you need to buy tissues? There are some provided at the hotel, in my room there are, anyway?"

"Yes, it's very comfortable, but there are tissues and tissues. I needed these special moisturising ones. I heard someone mention about the steam train, in the bar, and decided I'd try and see it. Then I went on to the supermarket. Were you just going out for a walk?"

"Yes."

"No special reason?"

"No."

"Funny, I got the impression you were following me, why?"

"Not at all. Why would I want to do that?"

"Probably because my uncle asked you to. Enjoy your walk, which way are you going?"

"I was going to see what is up here."

"I'm not, I'm going back to my room."

Having successfully shaken him off, she had a look round the town centre, before going back to the pub. She heard him come back to his room about half an hour after she did. She also heard the distinct chink of a bottle.

Tim Royce was a steam enthusiast, and had walked to the station to see the train. He decided to call into the Lion for a pint before going home, and was well known there. He parked himself at the corner of the bar, and spoke to his namesake, Tim White, who was serving the few drinkers in the pool room. He asked about Greywell, and before long, Cecil came down, demanding tea was served there. Tim Royce looked at the group, and watched them go into the dining room. Thoughtfully, he left his glass and walked home. He rang Brenda when he got home, but she was out, so he left a message on her Ansaphone.

Archie Babble was also watching the group, as they went into the dining room. Not only did he know who they were, but he had reason to hate Cecil with a vengeance. Archie had changed a lot over the past twenty-five years. His thick thatch of blonde hair had gone, he was now bald, and having worked on the roads for years, he was wrinkled and weather tanned. No longer did he look like the Adonis he had once been. His grievance with Cecil had festered in his mind over the years.

Archie had, unfortunately, had rather a lot to drink. Here was his opportunity, at last. 'All comes to him who wait,' was his thought, as he waited by the dining room door.

Cecil walked out of the double doors, loudly demanding to know where Ted and Jim were, and announced that he was to be informed the moment they arrived. He turned to find Archie in his path.

"Hello Cecil, remember me, do you?"

"No, is there any reason why I should? Get out of my way you drunken ape! You stink of booze."

"Well I remember you, and what you did to me and mine. Everybody, do you know who this crook is? He pretended to befriend us, twenty-five years ago, said he was a financial consultant and mortgage broker. All he did was con us all out of our savings, ruined me and others, caused untold misery."

Archie was shouting to a now silent bar.

"He offered to lend me the money to set up the filling station and garage, pressed me to go with him, said he'd look after me, and then when I began paying back, it was never enough. I paid him everything I had, but still he kept putting the rates up, showed me the small print, where it said he could, in exceptional circumstances. The only thing exceptional was his greed! I went bankrupt in a year, after he'd had my house, my business and the garage off me. He sold them for half they were worth. My fiancée left me, and my life was wrecked. I never got back on my feet. You all know me, I've worked on the council since then, good old Archie, will do anything for anyone. I even begged you to give me time, but no, you enjoyed hurting all of us. Now at last, I meet you face to face. I've waited a long time for this, you bastard. Now you can beg me, beg for your life, you unspeakable shit!"

Archie put his huge, work-worn hands round Cecil's throat, lifted him up, and shook the man, and squeezed. He was rapidly overpowered, and pulled off, and hustled out of the back door. Tim White and two hefty regulars managed to send him on his way. Back in the bar, Cecil was unable to say anything, but was red in the face. He was being attended to by Percy and Wilfred. Patrick came in from the other bar, and helped him up the stairs, and Cecil could be heard saying, "Babble, I'll sort him out again. Get the police here now, I wish to make a complaint."

Patrick called the station and was put through to Skipton. Within half an hour, two officers arrived, and while one went up to see Cecil, the woman officer asked for witnesses. She was almost swamped with offers to tell her all about it. What she was told had little resemblance to the truth, however. Archie's actions were more than justified, she was assured. Those who didn't take Archie's side, refused to say anything at all. Not one witness would or could back up his allegation, even Tim White, who said he didn't see what started it. The Pc came downstairs, and conferred with the woman officer. Pc Harper had not been successful either. He had a statement of complaint from Cecil, but the rest of his party had still been in the dining room when the assault had happened, and their evidence was of no use. Names and addresses were taken, and they left. Cecil had also complained of damage to his dentures that had become dislodged during his shaking. Patrick was able to direct him to Tim Royce, as the nearest local dentist.

Tim White soon calmed things down in the bar, and told all of them off, for joining ranks and refusing to say what had really happened. Then he bought the half dozen of them a drink. They all laughed. Naturally, it was the topic of conversation for some time.

Ted walked from the train station to the pub and quietly told Tim White who he was. He collected his key and met Jim on his way up the stairs. Half an hour later, in walked Greville and his family. Once the whole group had collected in the Writing Room, Cecil took the head of the table, and the proceedings were adjourned until the chairs were changed round to his satisfaction. Miles was recording the whole meeting, and Colin had a sheaf of papers ready to hand round. Cecil appeared little the worse for his assault, and after grumbling that everyone had taken their time arriving, he began.

"I have called you all here because I want you to know how I intend to conduct the family business from this time on. Most of you I have found wanting in many respects and it is time I did something about it. I no longer intend to subsidise your expensive habits and lifestyles, and will not do so. At the end of this week, I shall be signing my new will. I have no intention of shuffling off this mortal coil for some years, but after a mild heart attack last year, I have decided it only right to tell you how things will stand. I do value those who are truly loyal, and can be of use to me."

"As you know, I am a very rich man, which I became by being clever and working hard to get what I wanted. Those of you who can prove to me that you can do the same, may get something to help you. So no one is in any doubt about it, I will tell each of you where you stand. I shall begin with you, Greville, as you are my brother. I helped you to get started. Always, when you were in trouble, financial or otherwise, you have come crawling back for more, money, usually. I have pulled many strings for you, many times. I still own half your jewellery business, and now offer you the opportunity to buy me out. If you are unwilling or unable to do so, then I shall dissolve the business. Over the next few days we shall discuss this, and you can tell me how you will pay me back. The business is thriving now, so I know you can afford it.

"Ruby, you will get nothing from me. If you are short of cash, then sell the many items of jewellery you flaunt so easily, that, I may add, were taken without my permission, from the stock of the business, and are effectively half mine. You flaunt your wealth, so be prepared to pay for it.

"Melanie, you have your own source of income, which I consider to be a shame on the whole family. Some time ago, you came to me begging me to help set up a flat for you. You neglected to tell me that it was to be used for immoral purposes. How you have remained free from prosecution, I do not know. The time has come for you to buy your own flat now, so you can hand that one back to me, as you have not paid me one cent of rent, which you promised to do. I have no moral judgement or objection to your profession. I am hardly a man of strict morals myself, but you will not risk any connection to this family in future.

"Samantha, you have never actually asked me for anything, instead you took what you thought you could get away with. I rather admire that in a way. What disgusts me is the ease with which you allow yourself to be caught. At this very moment, I have arranged for the things of mine that are in your flat, to be returned. One of my men is working on that now. What you haven't had the sense to dispose of will be returned to me. I know exactly what you have taken over the last couple of years, and its value. You never seem short of money, I've had you watched. I know how you get your money, and as you seem to be in a career of drug pushing, you can pay me what you owe me. We also will talk about that during this week.

"Next, I come to you, Jim. You are my wife's brother, and as such, I expect you thought you would benefit from my will. Do you think I don't know how she ran to you, in the early years, to avoid her duties to me? You encouraged her to avoid me. I'll put my cards on the table, you tried hard to prevent me from marrying her, and hid her from me, and did all in your power to get her to leave me. I know all about you, and your rather interesting, if not illegal, activities. I also know that you have certain documents and information recorded somewhere, that I think I want, and for which I am prepared to pay you a fair price."

Jim stared at Cecil from the other end of the table.

"No Cecil, I don't think so. The only reason you have never come after me before is that you knew I had evidence about how my twin sister died. You see, I know. What is worrying you is that I have never seen fit to use it. What has changed, to make you so nervous now? As long as I have that hidden, but available, should anything happen to me, it is safe. I don't deal in blackmail, Cecil, unlike you. As long as I have what I do, about all of you, leave the women in your family alone. Was it not enough to rape your own sister, and others? Shall I go on? I know why Alana won't stay alone in your house. I have eyes and ears. I actually care about some of you, which is why I am here, to ensure you keep your hands, and other parts of your anatomy to yourself. You ever force yourself on anyone again, and I'll kill you. I have little to lose. No, I want no money from you. You called this meeting, and now I am here, I will have my say. Just know that what I know will always be there, ready to come to light, if required."

There was a stunned silence, for some minutes. Jim got up and left the room, saying, "I have little interest in listening to you belittle and deride the rest of the family, amusing as some of it might be. I have already arranged to pay my own charges here, and will stay here until this little jaunt is over, in case I am needed by any of your poor slaves, and to see fair play. If anyone wants me, I shall be down in the bar. Don't bother searching my room, there is nothing of use to any of you in it."

No matter how much Cecil screamed at him to come back, Jim had left the room. After fifteen minutes the meeting resumed. Windle had to fetch a drink from the bar for Cecil, to calm him down.

"Now we will deal with you, Alana. I actually like you quite a lot, and respect you. You have done well, and if you agree not to entangle yourself with Miles here, I am prepared to make you a substantial beneficiary of my will, but I would emphasise, that you cannot marry in my lifetime without my permission and approval. I have no intention of settling my fortune on some pathetic ne'er do well that you choose to have an affair with. That is the condition."

"Not only is that a quite unenforceable condition, Uncle Cecil, I don't give a damn what you do, and want none of your money. If I understood Jim correctly, I am not likely to accept any more gifts from someone who raped my mother, his own sister! Whatever hold you have on Miles, I don't know, or even want to, but you don't dictate to me who I may or may not see! Take your spies off me, beginning with Windle here, who seems to think he can follow me and spy on me. I'm glad Jim realises what you are like. You abused me, and for that alone, I should like to kill you. Maybe Jim will save me the bother. Mum, is it true?"

Her mother was shaking, and as white as a sheet. Ted was standing with his hand on her shoulder. Wilfred left the room hurriedly, and dashed to the bathroom just down the corridor.

"I cannot talk about this now, please leave it. No, it's not true, of course it isn't."

"Then let's get on. Ted, you have never liked me, or supported me or done anything but be aloof and condemning. I paid for your not inexpensive education and training, and now I would like a return on my investment. When can you pay me back for all that?"

"As soon as the banks open, and I can arrange a loan to meet the cost. I would leave now, except I think my mother and sister may need my support. You obscene little man. You pervert! Mum, is Wilf his, not Dad's?"

His mother sat, shaking her head. The tension in the room was almost overpowering.

"While you all exercise you overactive imaginations, I mean to finish what I have to say. Percy, you are an almost spineless wimp. You already know what to expect from me. So does Wilfred. Julia, you have been a loyal and good woman, and have looked after me very well. I have always made provision for you, and in the new will, I intend to leave you the house, and an adequate income for you to be comfortable, in recognition of your services. It will, of course, be in trust, as you are quite incapable of managing money, and that trust will be managed by Wilfred and Mr Windle here, or his appointed successor. Should you remarry, then the money will go to something else. I don't intend for someone else to live in luxury by latching on to you."

Julia had never been so angry, but years of resisting the impulse to argue had conditioned her to remain silent. Her eyes, behind their spectacles, flashed in anger, and she was shaking with fury, but she was determined to hear the rest of his plans so she said nothing.

Cecil pumped himself up, and after staring her out, he turned to Miles.

"You know why I keep you on, and if you wish to remain in my employ, then stop trying to see my niece. If you continue to do so, you know what will happen. Do I make myself clear?"

"Quite clear, sir. Please take a week's notice. I happen to love your niece, and hope she will one day do me the honour of becoming my wife."

"You have to give me a month's notice, it is in the contract, and you will work it, I insist."

"Then maybe you had better pay me what was in the contract, instead of the amount you have been paying. I am also owed several days' holiday."

"Yes, that's as maybe, but you are not going to insist, are you? I'm sure you don't want me to get talkative, do you?"

"Not particularly, no, but I'll not be blackmailed by you any more. I shall find a way to solve it. Several things spring to mind."

"Poppycock! I'll accept your apology when you have had time to think things through. Colin, I trust you are not going to turn on me? I can count on you, can't I? I intend to reward those who are loyal to me. I'll see you and your father all right, you know I will."

Colin blushed, and nodded, but looked down at the floor, and as soon as Cecil had looked away, Colin looked at Cecil with a look of real hatred, seen by Ted and Julia.

"Now, Bill, you will get the car, and the cottage you now live in, and an allowance. Charlie, you will be similarly rewarded. This is on the undertaking that you will keep all my affairs confidential, for the rest of your lives. Oliver, you have been my friend and faithful servant for many years. I have recompensed you adequately, bearing in mind that I know only too well that you have been creaming off large sums of money. Continue to do so, and I shall leave you a case of Lifebuoy soap, and some washing powder and a supply of flannels, and one case of cheap whiskey. If you wish to continue working for me, I want that money back, and then I will revise my will. Before you all go off to the bar, let me tell you that a copy of my proposed will is lodged at my home, in safety, with information helpful to the police, should I come to an unexpected death. There are copies of what I propose in these folders, one for each of you. Now, I shall go and have that delicious dinner I ordered, and if you don't want to pay for your own, you will join me. We will have another meeting in two days' time, and tomorrow, I shall tell you what times I will talk to each of you. Freshen up, dinner is in twenty minutes. Colin, ring the police, and find out if that oaf Babble has been locked up yet."

Chapter Four

Brenda was a few minutes later than her normal seven o'clock, as she hurried in to work on the Monday morning. She had enjoyed her weekend, and had not got back until very late, which was why she had overslept. She was still first in, however. Luke instantly demanded feeding, and she then tackled the enormous pile of laundry, before Elaine joined her in the main bar, which was remarkably clean. Patrick was doing breakfasts, and Wendy was in charge of the dining room. She grimaced, and said, "The whole lot have booked their breakfasts for eight sharp. They should be down any time now. I'll be glad to see the back of most of them, funny lot. The old man complains about everything, and only a few of them seem nice. The chap in room twelve is all right though. He stayed in the bar quite late last night, with the woman from room one, and her mother from room six, and the young man from room seven. He actually opened a door for me, when I was carrying a tray, and he helped me clear the bar after we had closed. He's a real gent."

Brenda was in the bar when the group came down in dribs and drabs. She was interested, and looked at each one as they came down the stairs. First down was Oliver Windle, who silently slithered into the dining room without acknowledging her "Good Morning."

He was followed by Miles and Colin, who smiled and passed her as she was polishing the tables. Next came Julia, Alana and Ted, who all smiled, and commented on how lovely the brasses looked, and how smart everything was. Then came Wilfred and Percy. Brenda looked at them, and had a shock. They both looked a lot like her but she moved aside to let them past. Percy looked up at her, and smiled. They stared at each other for some time, before he hurried into the dining room. Then Cecil came down with Greville and his family. He totally ignored Brenda, but she looked at him long and hard. Bill scurried down the stairs after them, and he was followed by Charlie, who walked stiffly and had the beginnings of a black eye, and a bad scratch on his face.

Brenda got on with cleaning the Ladies, while Elaine did the Gents, and then they polished the door plates. As she put Brasso on the dining room door plates, Brenda looked carefully at the group at breakfast. A rather unpleasant idea was forming in her head. She could hear Cecil demanding to know where Jim was, and then complaining about the scrambled eggs.

Brenda and Elaine went up a little later, and as usual started with room twelve. Brenda knocked on the door twice, as she could hear the television still on. She let herself in with the pass key; the curtains were closed, a bedside light was on, and a book was open on the bedside table. The bed had been laid on, but not in. There was no one in the room, and no one in the bathroom. There was a full bath run, but when she felt it, it was cold. The bathroom light was also on. It looked as if someone had been called away unexpectedly during the night. There was a wallet on the bedside table, and a mobile phone, and an unfinished drink, whiskey from the smell of it, beside the open book. A hardly-smoked cigarette had been stubbed out in the ashtray, and the packet and lighter were still there. It was so odd, that she called Elaine in, and they checked the whole room. None of the towels had been used, although one had been moved.

They tidied the room, let the bath run out, cleaned the bathroom, and tidied the bed, before closing the door. Room eleven was untidy, the bathroom was strewn with make up, and the ashtrays were full. It took some time to clean and when they had done that room, they moved on to room ten. It was neither tidy nor clean, but apart from a pile of cheap magazines, the only thing unusual was the mass of jewellery on the table. There were several empty glasses from the bar in the rooms, so Brenda took them down to the bar, and spoke to Patrick about room twelve, before joining Elaine in room seven. This was tidy, and easily cleaned. Room nine was opposite room seven, and obviously used by two people. One of the pillowcases, when they turned it over, was soaked in blood, and they had to change it. Elaine suggested that the person must have had a nose bleed.

Room six was tidy, and room eight was not. They cleaned both of them, and then took a brief break downstairs, to reload the washing machines. Elaine was called away to order materials for the next week, and Brenda knocked on the door of room five, with some trepidation. A voice from the Writing Room next door called, "Go on in, my dear, it is all ready for you to clean."

Brenda found the room was meticulously tidy, with neat piles of paperwork on the table. She swiftly stripped the bed, and started to clean the bathroom, when Cecil came into the room. He stood in the doorway, and looked at her. She looked up at him, and wondered what he intended. With a charming smile, he said, "My dear, I see you know I need clean bedding. Good attention to detail. I'm impressed. You seem to know what you are doing."

She finished cleaning the bath, and stood up.

"Thank you sir, do you need anything extra, teas, coffee, soaps?"

"No, I have all I require. You remind me very much of a chambermaid that was here many years ago. Feisty lass she was, she was prettier than you, but you have the same eyes. How old are you?"

"Twenty-four, sir. If you will excuse me, I need to get on, and fetch your clean bedding."

"Certainly, child. Could you do the Writing Room next, and could I ask for a standard lamp in there?"

"Yes, sir, I'll get you one. If you need a blotter or ink, they are in the drawer of the sideboard in there."

"Well, I thank you, that will be helpful."

He stood aside, and as she finished the bathroom, she was aware he was watching her, with amused interest. As she passed the marble topped table, she accidentally knocked a file off, and its contents fell on the floor. She picked them up, and noticed several photographs amongst the papers, and glanced briefly at them. She paused, and stared at several of them, before putting them back in the file. She looked up at Greywell, and said, "I'm so sorry, sir."

He replied, "Not to worry, they are not important. I was going to tidy them up anyway."

He had a strange smile on his face that rather unnerved her. He was watching her, with some amusement.

Elaine came back, and they made the bed together, and Brenda vacuumed while Elaine cleaned the Writing Room, and Brenda did the communal bathroom next door. Cecil went back to the Writing Room, and Elaine joined her.

"I think the man from room nine had most of his nose bleed in there. The sink is covered in blood. There is some on the floor, too. He's tried to wash it away, but not very well."

"Yes, the bin is full of bloody loo roll. I'll do it."

"All right, I'll go and start in room one, then."

Brenda made a thorough job of cleaning the bathroom, and when she had finished, she remembered she had left polish in the Writing Room. She walked in, and saw Cecil at the table, writing.

"Sorry to disturb you sir, I left the polish in here. You have everything you need?"

"Thank you, young lady, I do. Here, you have done well, you and the older woman. Take this."

As she passed, he pressed a note in her hand. She said, "Thank you, sir, I'm glad you are comfortable."

He had a very mischievous, but quite appealing smile, which made her nervous as she fled out of the room. By the time she got to the back corridor, she had seen the note was a ten. She showed it to Elaine.

"Put it in the pot, Elaine, we can all share it."

"He's taken a shine to you, why?"

"I don't know, he seems to hate everyone else. Mum told me to be very careful of him. If you don't mind, I'd rather you were there if I do that room again. He makes me very nervous."

"Fine, I will be."

Room two not only smelled of unwashed person, the bath had not been used, and there was an empty whiskey bottle and a glass on the floor. The sheets of the bed were grubby, so they changed them, and after opening the window, they sprayed the room with air freshener, before moving on to the other rooms.

By one, the cleaning was done, and Brenda was able to get home for a couple of hours, before returning to work behind the bar from three until seven. Cecil came over to her, and said, "You do work hard, girl. Do you never get time off?"

"Oh, yes sir. I had the whole weekend off."

"What did you do with it?"

"I played for our local hockey team on Saturday, away at Kendal, and yesterday I went paragliding. It was cold, but the wind was just right. I do quite a lot of that, and caving."

"Quite a remarkable young woman, all in all. Is your father proud of you?"

"I doubt it, I never knew him, or anything about him; my stepfather is my father, really. Yes, I hope he is."

"Do you still live at home?"

"No, I have no wish to be a burden on my parents. I have my own little place. They have my brothers to look after. Since I left school I have always paid my way. I may well be illegitimate, but I am still too proud to sponge off anyone!"

"Quite admirable. Can I buy you a drink?"

"Thank you, sir, but I never drink while I am working, if I do, I tend to make mistakes."

"Is your mother Doreen Williams?"

"She was, but she is Doreen Royce now. She married the local dentist."

"Yes, I am seeing him this afternoon, in about fifteen minutes, actually. So that's your stepfather, is it? I think I knew your mother, when I stayed here before. We didn't part on the best of terms, probably better not to mention it to her."

Cecil asked her how to get to the surgery, and set off. Brenda was confused. This man, who everyone else seemed to find intolerable, was trying very hard to be pleasant to her. She wondered what his motives were. She was not sure what to do. When he returned to the pub, he went upstairs, and apart from him winking at her when he came through the bar, she didn't see him again that day.

She went from the pub to her mother's home and was glad to find her stepfather alone there. Her mother was at a singing rehearsal, for the Operatic carol concert, and her brothers were at Scouts.

"Dad, I have a problem, and I need your advice. I think there is something I need to know, but I know that if I ask Mum she will get very upset. Do you know who my real father is?"

"I think so, yes. I didn't until recently, but I think you have worked it out, same as I have. What has your mother told you?"

"That I was the result of a one night stand, that my real father had left long before she knew she was pregnant, and that as she wanted nothing more to do with him, she decided to bring me up on her own, that she hated him. I gave up asking ages ago, because every time I did, she got so upset. I love her very much, but now, I think I need to know. I think it is very important. You are my father, you brought me up, you and Mum."

"Yes, that is what we agreed she would tell you, because she never wanted you to know what really happened. You were the result of her being forced, against her will. Effectively she was raped, but things got so bad for her, she was persuaded not to press charges. If she could put that out of her mind, then she could love you. She wasn't a virgin, and they found all her previous boyfriends, and so she couldn't bear all that a trial would have revealed, and when I met and fell in love with her, which I still am, deeply, I was only too happy to accept you as my daughter. Now you know, or think you know who he is, don't you?"

"I think it is this Major Greywell. I spoke to him today, and he looks rather like me, and so do his two sons. I saw them this morning; it was like looking in a funny mirror. I think he knows, too. He is being ever so nice to me. I don't know what to do now."

"Yes, I came to the same conclusion when I saw him yesterday. Keep your distance, if you can. He is certainly not to be trusted. When I think what he put your mother through, all those years ago, I would like to do him very serious harm. He came to my surgery today, he said he'd spoken to you, and asked a lot of questions about you and your mother. I told him very little. Do you want to get to know him?"

"No. I've seen the way he treats his family. I hate him, for what he did to Mum. Dad, where did the money come from that Mum gave me on my twenty-first birthday, that paid for my house?"

"So you have worked that out, have you? All right, when your mother agreed not to pursue her complaint of rape, he offered her a lot of money. She wanted none of it, but she was in one hell of a jam, when she found out she was pregnant. She refused to tell him, she was afraid he might claim some sort of rights over you. He had sent the money via a third party. She was desperate, so she took it. It was a lot of money then, and she lived off the interest, until I came along. We discussed it, and she decided to settle it on you, when you were old enough to be sensible about it, which you have been. He never knew anything about it. What are you going to do?"

"I think the money should go to her."

"No, I don't. She gave it to you, and she is happier that she did. I hate him too, and would like to beat his brains out, but it would only upset Doreen, which I will do anything to prevent. Just be very careful what you tell him, please. I don't want her meeting him, or him knowing where she lives. It would be foolish to tell him where you live, either!"

"No way. I'm glad I know, but I won't talk to Mum about it. I love her too much to put her through that. If she ever asks, will you tell her I know, and I would never change anything she did for me? I wish there was some way I could make him suffer, without involving Mum."

"There is, I already have it in hand. Leave it with me. He told me something today, deliberately, I think. He is making a new will, and said the whole of his family hate him, most of them with good reason. He is testing them all. He has already made a will, it is at his home, locked away. The only ones he has any time for are those who told him to go to hell, the ones who stand up for themselves, and are independent of him. He said the rest of them were spongers, and he can't stand them. He said he had done many evil things in his life, which he regrets, and now he wants to make up for them. I think he was, in a roundabout way, asking me to tell you how sorry he was that he never knew about you. He said he thought you were a fine young woman. He is booked in again for the morning, do you want me to tell him anything?"

"Yes, tell him to go to hell! I've managed my life this far without him, I don't need him now, or his money. Can you do that?"

"Yes, I can."

Brenda went home, thought about it, and then decided to pretend the whole thing did not worry her. After two cups of tea, she went to bed.

Chapter Five

Brenda was a little nervous when the group came down to breakfast the next morning. The man with the black eye didn't show, but the others were rather silent, except for Cecil, who acknowledged her before going into the dining room. She was rather grateful that he didn't come over to her and try to talk. She was just finishing vacuuming the main bar, having already done the pool room, and she was having difficulty persuading the cat to move away from the big old settle by the fireplace. Luke was scratching the carpet in front of it, and behaving rather oddly. In the end, she put him outside until he calmed down. There was a faintly sweet aroma in the main bar, not unpleasant, and she wondered what had been smoked in there the night before.

When she and Elaine got up to room twelve, they found it was exactly as they had left it the day before. Both of them felt uneasy, and went to talk to Patrick about it. He asked them to see if the room keys were in the room, and after a search, they went back to him, to say the room keys were missing. Patrick asked to speak to Major Greywell, which he did in the Writing Room. He came back to room twelve, and told them, "No one has seen him since the night before last. He had paid for the room for the whole week. Major Greywell suggests if he doesn't turn up by tomorrow morning, then he will report him missing. They did have a big family row, and he may have gone back to his home, and be returning. He is going to ring his house, see if he is there. He also mentioned that one of the two men in room nine seems to have disappeared overnight."

"The one with the black eye? Who had the nose bleed all over the pillow, and must have bled in the bathroom as well?"

"Did he? Yes, he did have a black eye. The other chap in there says he never came up from the bar last night. His keys are missing, too."

Major Greywell did not seem unduly worried that two of his party were unaccounted for. He left the pub just after nine, and visited the solicitors over the bank opposite the pub, and from there he kept his appointment with the dentist. Tim Royce had fixed his dentures, and with little conversation, he left, having paid the bill in cash. As he left, he said, "When the time is appropriate, could you give someone a message for me?"

"So long as it will not hurt anyone, yes, I will."

"Would you tell my daughter that I admire her, and respect her, and her mother? I never knew, if I had, I would have looked after her. I cannot undo what was done, nor do I want to cause any distress. I have left provision for her in my new will. One day she will be a rich woman."

"I will."

"It is her independence and willingness to work hard that I admire. I'm not a very pleasant or kind man, so I shall not risk polluting her by trying to get to know her. Should she ever ask, tell her that she is the best thing I think I've ever created, mainly because I wasn't around to wreck her."

"If she asks, I will tell her. I doubt she will."

Back at the pub, Cecil went up to his room, and then went back to the solicitor. He decided to have a walk around the town, so he called Miles and Ted, and asked them to accompany him. They ended up on the top of the Castleberg Rock, which overlooked the town. It was quite a stiff climb up there, and Cecil sat on the seat for some time getting his breath back. Miles stood back, and Ted said, "I saw the bank manager today. Here is the cheque for the amount I estimate you paid for my education. I have not included interest, are you going to demand it?"

Cecil looked at Ted. He took the cheque that Ted was holding out, and looked at it.

"Well done, lad, you have passed my test. I know you hate my guts, with good reason. I've done many bad things in my life. This is what I intend to do with this cheque."

Cecil tore the cheque into a dozen small pieces, put them in a pile on the ground and set fire to them with his cigar lighter.

"Ted, you owe me nothing. Things are not always what they seem, you know. My only advice for you is not always to believe everything you are told, especially by your nearest and dearest. Miles, go back to the hotel, and Ted and I will follow. I need to talk to him, in private. If nothing else, I owe him an explanation."

The two of them sat for over an hour, talking, until it was lunchtime. After lunch Cecil went back once more to the solicitor, and spent some time there. Ted went for a long walk that afternoon. He walked beside the river Ribble for some way, and when he reached a small village, retraced his steps. There were woods coming down to the river, and the path went through them. He turned a corner, and was startled to hear his mother's voice, talking to someone, from a small clearing. He crept forward to see who it was. His mother was not one to indulge in country walks, especially not in wet weather, and he was a little startled to see that the person with her was Greville. He could not pass without them seeing him, and it was obvious that they were deep in a very private conversation. He watched as his mother handed Greville a packet, which he put in his pocket.

Ted walked back to the village, found a way over the river across a weir, and walked back along the road. He came to a turning leading to the village of Langcliffe, and decided to investigate. The village green was pretty, and he found the small but well equipped Post Office, where he purchased some tissues and a chocolate bar, and walked back to join the main road. As he headed down the hill towards Settle, he saw a couple walking ahead of him, and realised it was Percy and his sister. As she had always professed to dislike Percy, and they were deep in conversation, he didn't want to walk with them, so he took the first turn left, and walked along a winding country lane, until he came down into the market square from above the town. It was too late to go into the bank, so he went back to his room and thought for a while, before going down to the bar and having a drink. By supper time he was moderately drunk.

Miles looked for Alana after lunch, and was rather distressed when he saw her leave with Percy. Instead of an afternoon spent with her, he decided to try and talk to Cecil.

He found him in the Writing Room. They had a long talk, which became heated, and in the end he stormed out, saying, "I don't give a damn what you do any more. You will regret this, I promise."

As he turned towards his room, he almost bumped into the police sergeant. Adrian Graves moved back to let Miles pass, and then knocked on the door of the Writing Room.

"Good afternoon, Major Greywell, can I have a few minutes of your time?"

"By all means, officer, I trust you have arrested that idiot Babble?"

"That is why I am here."

Miles was quite unashamed at bolting into his room and straining to hear what was said. He heard Cecil shouting, and the more calm, measured tones of the large policeman. Eventually, the conversation resumed normal levels, and the policeman left. He was waiting for Cecil to summon him, and came as soon as he was called.

"Yes, you called?"

"Did none of you see what that idiot Babble did and said to me?"

"I heard some of it, yes, but I was still in the dining room. That was all I could tell the police, sir."

"How convenient! Very well. I want to talk to my brother, Greville, get him for me please, I'll see him in here."

Greville was nowhere to be found in the hotel, and nor was Ruby. Miles was unable to find either of the daughters, and told Cecil so.

"Then fetch my sister and Alana please."

Miles couldn't find them, either. With some trepidation he told Cecil, who said, "In which case, I shall go to my room and rest for an hour. When they do come in, tell them to wait for me in here."

Percy was feeling very uneasy. The dawning realisation that Wilfred was his brother, rather than just his cousin, made him feel very insecure. He had been controlled and browbeaten by his father for so long, that he had no confidence in himself, and believed that he was far from intelligent. His early attempts to gain his father's respect had always ended in disaster. What Alana had told him that afternoon, had confirmed his suspicion that Wilfred had sabotaged most of his plans, and tried to make him look a fool when around his father.

Julia knew that something was troubling Ted, something to do with her. She wondered just what Cecil had told him, on the walk they had been on earlier. She was so worried that she had asked Greville to help her. Greville had his uses, including a wide acquaintance with the less salubrious underworld. Julia could not afford for the truth about her and Cecil to get out. Her brother had never pretended to have morals or any great degree of honesty or integrity, but she had always set store by her reputation. Cecil had never pushed her into a corner to this degree before. She knew him for what he was, always had done. When her husband had been serving overseas, she had accepted his invitation to give her and the children a home, in the full knowledge that there would be a price. One she had paid willingly. Now she had to keep what she had, and was not prepared to lose it. She had to act fast, and be ruthless. She sat in her room, and thought.

Brenda finished working in the bar at about eight that evening. Almost all Cecil's party was in the bar. Cecil was sat by the roaring fire, talking to Greville and Ruby. They seemed to be having an argument. Brenda couldn't stop looking at them. She was relieved when the bar manager, John, told her to get off home, and that he and Tim could cope. What unnerved her most was the creepy, rather smelly big slob of a man, from room two, who was quietly knocking back the whiskeys and was watching everyone and everything. He was very difficult to hear, he seemed to whisper all the time. A party of locals came into the pool room as she prepared to go. She recognised Jack and Jo

Atterthwaite, and the policeman, Adrian Graves, and an older man who looked very like him. As she left she heard Adrian call him 'Dad'. She collected her coat and slunk out of the back door, then up through the market place, where she met a friend of hers, Colleen. After a brief chat, she agreed to go over to the Royal Oak for a quick drink.

It was about nine when she left her friend, and walked up the hill to go home. There was an excellent television programme on when she got in, and when that had finished, she cooked a meal, fed the cats, and settled down. By bed time, she was still very much awake, and couldn't settle. She kept thinking of Cecil, and whether he was in fact her father. Logic told her that she didn't need him, or to get to know him, but emotion told her that she was interested, and wanted to know more. She also felt guilty that she was betraying her mother and stepfather by wanting to. It seemed disloyal to them, to want more than they had given her. Even a milky drink had no effect, so well after midnight she looked out of the window, trying to calm her mind. She was surprised to see it was starting to snow. Almost on an impulse, she grabbed a warm coat and hat, and gloves, and went for a walk.

She headed out of town, up towards the hills. She knew every step, and did not need a torch. She climbed up the stony lane behind the town, and when she got to the end of the lane, by the old ruined building, she noticed the snow was getting deeper. She sheltered for a while in the lee of the building, and then walked on, not going up the steep climb, but towards the village of Langcliffe. There was a strange, rather eerie silence of the soft snow, that was settling thickly on the ground. Twice she slipped, but the snow cushioned her fall. The blizzard was getting much worse, and she knew that to go higher or further afield was foolish. It was further to go back, than forward, to reach a proper road, so she made her way carefully down to the village and found the road, with difficulty.

The village green at Langcliffe was always pretty, but from what she could see in the snow, it looked tranquil and beautiful under its white blanket. It was well past two when she trudged into the edge of town, and still feeling very awake, she went to the bridge over the Ribble, and watched the snow building on the river banks.

There was no traffic around, and no tyre tracks on the road, so she was very startled when a voice behind her said, "I hope you are not considering jumping? Are you all right?"

The man behind her was the police sergeant, Adrian Graves. He was rather reassuring in his old fashioned cape, and his great size made her feel safe. He held a torch in his hand, and snow was heavy on his helmet, and over his shoulders.

"No, not at all, I'm fine. I couldn't sleep, I had some thinking to do, and I love the snow, so I came out. I do my best thinking outdoors, so I went over from Banks Lane to Langcliffe, as I couldn't get up to Attermire, the snow was too deep and it would have been foolish in these conditions. I suppose I'd better get home, I'm working in the morning."

"Yes, you work at the Brass Cat, don't you? I'll walk with you so far. Brenda, isn't it? It's funny, lots of people seem to be out tonight. I've already come across Jack Atterthwaite, and later his brother Jo, not to mention seeing Archie Babble hurrying down Station Road just now. Some of the guests from the Cat have been out and about, from the footprints to and from the back door. You would think on a wild night like this, folk would stay inside. I have to be out, well, no, I don't, I could be in the nick, catching up on paperwork, but police cars are grounded except in emergencies, and like you, I had some thinking to do. I still enjoy foot patrol when I can get out to do it."

They walked together towards the centre of town, and at the police station, Sergeant Graves said, "Will you be all right from here, or would you like me to see you to your door?"

"How kind of you, but I only live in Upper Settle, I'll be fine. Thank you for looking after me."

"Just get home safe, please. I'd better get in to do that paperwork. I'll just check down Station Road first, then I'll get inside."

He walked on and she saw him turn right down Station Road, and she turned left up by the police station yard, and at the end of the road she looked back. She was rather surprised to see a man walking in the road, and thought she was imagining it when she thought she recognised her stepfather, Tim Royce, walking towards the lower end of town. She thought about following him, but decided she must be mistaken, and hurried off to her home.

Adrian Graves checked the Railway Station, and round the back of the vet's as well as the cricket club, before heading back to the station. The snow was lying thick on the ground, and he was able to track his footprints, and those of Brenda, but was startled to see two sets of male prints leading from the Golden Lion, one towards the lower end of town, and another towards the town square, where they led to the road leading to the main car park. A call on the radio interrupted him, and he returned to the police station.

In her room in the hotel, Wendy woke during the night, because she could hear one or more guests moving around. She checked her watch, and saw it was just before three in the morning. After a few minutes, when the emergency bell had not been rung, she went back to sleep. Guests sometimes moved from room to room, for various reasons.

Chapter Six

Brenda overslept, but only by about fifteen minutes, and by rushing she made it through the snow, and to the Golden Lion by seven thirty-three. She arrived at the same time as Elaine, who had been delayed by taking her time walking very carefully down the slippery pavement. The snow was thick on the ground, and more was falling by the minute. Once inside they dealt with the laundry and started on the main bar. Wendy was sorting out breakfasts, and gradually the guests came down. Brenda looked for Cecil but he did not make an appearance.

There was a rather unpleasant smell in the main bar, especially by the fireplace. When Brenda polished the door handles, she noticed it in the telephone cupboard as well, and decided to ask Patrick to get the drains checked. The two of them finished downstairs earlier than normal, and Elaine said, "I'll sort the laundry out, if you go up and open the rooms up and get the dirty towels, and of course, room five's bedding."

Brenda happily went upstairs. Room twelve had not been touched, and she worked her way down the front corridor. There was no reply from room five, so she entered, and found that the bed had not been slept in. As she came out of the room, she noticed that, unusually, the Writing Room door was closed. She knocked, and when she received no reply, she went into the room.

Slumped over the table in the middle of the room was Cecil. There was blood all over the table, and the floor. That he was dead was obvious, but she had been trained in first aid, and cautiously approached, and could find no pulse. She made sure she didn't tread in the soggy blood on the carpet, and dashed out of the room, shutting the door behind her. She made it to the bathroom before she was violently sick. Something told her she should scream or have hysterics, but she couldn't. She almost went into auto pilot as she walked down to the main bar, and grabbed the telephone in the still room and rang 999. Wendy, hearing her talk on the phone, rushed to fetch Elaine from the laundry room, and when Brenda had calmly finished her phone call, they sat her in the main bar, on the settle, as she burst into tears. Patrick was soon found and told what had happened.

"The police say to let no one in until they get there, and to keep the door shut. I'm sorry, but I feel a bit shaky. Could I have a cup of coffee?"

"You can have more than that; Wendy, get her a brandy, quickly."

The police were there within minutes, and a detective went up to the Writing Room, and looked in. Not long after him was a doctor, who confirmed that Cecil was dead. Before long, the whole of the upper floor was sealed, and there were policemen swarming over the pub. Brenda sat with Elaine on the settle, both of them very quiet, and they waited to be spoken to. Pat hastily found keys for the Writing Room, and then shut the whole pub, locked the doors at the request of the police, and asked Wendy to make coffee for everyone. Brenda sat until she felt a little less sick, and then said, "I'm better now. What do you need me to do?"

"Stay there and sit tight, a detective is coming down to talk to you in a few minutes."

As Brenda sat, she became nauseated by the strange smell around her. As there was nothing else to do, she decided to investigate it. She got up, and looked around her and removed the cushions from the seat she had been sitting on, and lifted up the wooden seat of the old settle, half expecting to find a dead mouse inside. What she found made her drop the seat with a bang. She looked over at Elaine, and said, "I think you should get that detective here right now. There is another body in here. I think it's the man from room twelve, but I'm not sure. Why me?"

"In all the years I've been here, I had no idea that opened. Sit down before you fall over. Officer, come here, quickly, we've found another one."

Brenda was shaking and tearful when they got to her. She was taken to the dining room to sit down. She was in shock. She barely noticed anyone else around her. Policemen, fellow hotel workers, and guests were milling around. A policewoman came and sat with her. It took some time before she could become coherent. The doctor came and asked her if she needed a sedative. She said, "No, but could I ring my stepdad? I think I need him, or my mum, him preferably."

"Shall we ring him for you?"

"No, I'll do it. I'll use the public phone, all the others seem busy."

She got up, and shakily walked to the small cupboard by the front door, with the policewoman helping her. Once inside, they just squeezed in, and shut the door as it was noisy in the main bar. The sickly sweet smell of decay was almost overpowering.

"Not again!" she muttered, and looked around. She hesitantly opened the small access door from the telephone booth, that gave access to under the stairs. It was dark in there, and the policewoman produced a small torch from her pocket, and shone it into the dusty cupboard.

"God Almighty!" The policewoman shut the door quickly, and leaned against the wall, sweating and pale. "Look, just get out of here, and go and sit back in the dining room. I'll get control room to ring your stepfather."

"This is like a nightmare, please tell me I'm going to wake up from this!"

Once out of the telephone booth, Brenda was taken to the dining room, while the woman officer told the detective she had found yet another body in the cupboard under the stairs. Before long Brenda went with the policewoman to the police station, where she was allowed to sit in a quiet room, and given tea, until her stepfather turned up and sat with her while she explained what she had found. Her own doctor also attended, a man she had known all her life, and who she trusted. He insisted that she was taken home.

"My home, please, I want to lie down quietly, and cuddle my cats. I need to be alone for a bit."

"No, I don't want you alone, I want someone in the house with you. Shall I ask your mother to come?"

"No, if I must have someone, can you ask my friend, Colleen?"

She was taken home in a police car, and before long Colleen had arrived, made her hot, sweet tea, put her to bed, with a hot water bottle and found the two cats. The doctor had given her some tablets, one of which she took, and soon she was fast asleep.

Back at the pub, Elaine had mild hysterics, Wendy had to sit down, and Patrick wondered what he was going to do, as the pub was closed, and the guests were told they couldn't leave.

More police arrived, and he was wondering where to put everyone. On the upper story of the building was a large staff flat, currently unoccupied, so he put all the guests up there, and handed the main keys of the building over to the police, and went to his home, where he made a number of calls to his solicitor, insurers and his parents. This was not a situation that he had ever envisaged, and he had no idea what to do. It was obvious that he would need to assist the police, but his business was likely to fold.

Chapter Seven

Saul Catchpole was a quiet, rather imposing man in his early fifties, with a shock of ginger hair speckled with grey, and bright blue eyes. His freckled face was lined and weatherworn. He was looking out of the window of his dining room, at the blizzard that meant he couldn't go walking that day. His wife, Diana, was clearing the breakfast things, and his two daughters were huddled in a corner, discussing some pop star. His son Samuel came and stood beside him.

"Looks like walking is out for the day, Dad. Isn't it your day off, what are you going to do?"

"I think, if I can get into work, I'll go in and clear some of my paperwork. I'm sorry, son, but it would be downright stupid to walk in this. Are you very disappointed?"

"Yes, but it can't be helped. Er, Dad, can I bum a lift with you? I suppose I'd better do some Christmas shopping. I know what I'll get the girls, but I have no clue what I can get Mum."

"I see, but I think I might know, that CD of Bryn Terfel. I'm getting her something else."

"Fine, but, well never mind, I'll get it later in the week, then."

"How much do you need?"

"Thanks, Dad, I'll pay you back, I promise. I'm just a bit short at the moment."

Saul allowed himself a wry smile as they went out to the car, and got in. He handed over some notes from his wallet, and said, "Make your own way back from town, and when you get home you could clear all the snow from the drive, and the footpath outside, and then do Mrs Wilkinson next door? If you want to wash the car, and chop some logs, then we can reach a suitable price. Would that help a bit?"

"Not half, Dad! Thanks. I don't mean to cadge off you, but that bike costs a bit, since that last spill in the triathlon."

"I know. Just keep quiet about my giving you a sub, or the girls will want some, and I know for a fact they have plenty of cash that your auntie gave them recently. Did she not give you anything?"

"No. She said as I was now eighteen, I wasn't getting anything because I was a student, and would just spend it on drink or drugs! Why doesn't Aunty Ruth like me?"

"I expect for the same reason she doesn't like me. We are men, and she holds us in low esteem. No man is worthy of her admiration. She can be quite nasty, sometimes. She hates me for taking her sister from her. Diana told me that she has announced she is coming to us for Christmas. I thought of getting her a dildo for a present, but she would be furious, so I expect it will be bath salts or something. You'd better get her something too."

"I know what she would like, actually. She wants a metric spanner set so she can mend her motor bike, but I can't afford a good one, and unless I get her the best she will be right scathing about it."

"Then let's combine, and get her one, from the pair of us. Here take this, and get one. Get plain wrapping paper, or it will be politically incorrect or something. I'm getting your mother jewellery, could you stretch to a silver chain as well as a CD?"

"With what you just gave me, sure. Dad, your bleeper is going off, shall I cancel it for you?"

"Please. If it is work I shall have to ring in, so I'll pull over to do so."

When he had pulled over and stopped the car, he got out and walked to the side of the road, and called up on his mobile. He ran back to the car, got in, and swore.

"Sam, I'll have to drop you off on the edge of town. There is a triple murder come in at Settle."

"Settle? You are kidding! Nothing ever happens there. Nice town though. Good cricket team and rugby, too. Tell you what, can I come with you? I'll make my own way back."

"If you want to, either that, or you can bring the car back, and I'll get a lift or catch the train. If you want a well ordered life, son, don't be a policeman. I'm meant to be off for the next five days!"

"Do you want me to do some shopping for you? I know how long these murder cases take, and a triple one, it will mean we won't see you over the holidays at all. I can accept it's your job, but you do see that I'll have to cope with Auntie Ruth on my own? That's just not fair. Can I run away to sea?"

"I wouldn't wish that on anyone, but being the officer in charge of the murder squad does have its compensations! I'll think of something, I promise."

It took some time to drive to Settle. Sam went into town, while Saul went into the police station, and then to the pub. The scenes of crime technicians were already there, and the photographers. Saul was met by his deputy, Woman Detective Inspector Celia Allenby.

"Sir, this is a very strange one. There is a body in a piece of furniture, been there some days, one stuffed in an under-stairs cupboard, not, according to the police surgeon, quite so dead, and one freshly killed, last night, by the look of things, in the Writing Room upstairs. We know who two of them are, but not the one under the stairs, yet. We may have to knock a wall down to get him out. We think we know, but until someone can get a good look at him, which they can't at the moment, we cannot jump to any conclusions. This is Patrick Raistrick, the owner of the Golden Lion, and this is Detective Superintendent Saul Catchpole."

Saul shook hands with Patrick, and then put on a white plastic goon suit, before going into the bar. He looked first at the body in the wooden settle. It had signs of decomposition, and smelled bad.

"We know who this is?"

"Yes, sir. A James Arthur Cordwell. Ex-army, and the brother-in-law to the dead man upstairs. He disappeared several days ago, after a family row. No apparent next of kin, that we can find at the moment, apart from some of the other guests here, who are all upstairs in the staff flat, where I understand they are squabbling like children."

"I see, show me this cupboard." Saul changed into a fresh goon suit, and was shown the telephone booth.

Saul peered into the small door in the wall of the telephone booth. With a powerful torch he saw the crumpled body of a man, lying on its face, and having apparently been pushed in and left. He assessed the size of the door, and coming out of the telephone cupboard, said, "There is no way I could even get into that hole. I'm too big. He must have been quite a slight chap. Get the wall taken down. Who do we think he is?"

"We think he is a Charles Alphonse Grimsdale. Known as Charlie, he was the general assistant and handyman to Cecil Greywell, who is the man upstairs. Grimsdale has a brother somewhere; the secretary, Miles something is looking it up for us."

"Well done, I'd better get another suit, and look at the one upstairs. Who is he?"

"Major Cecil Wilfred Nelson Greywell. Date of birth, 7th December 1938. Greywell House, Wall Road, York. Occupation, company director. He was in the Royal Engineers, and then went into business as a financial director. Most of his family are already here, they were having some sort of a family conference here. He was not, apparently, the most popular of men, not only with his family, but a lot of locals as well."

Saul was shown to the Writing Room, and went in and looked at the body of Cecil. Having confirmed that forensics had been completed, he looked closer, and saw that the corpse had a cut throat, from which a vast quantity of blood had poured over the table, down onto the carpet and over another chair. After a quick look round Saul went back downstairs, and in the pool room he conferred with the medical examiner and his gathering team of detectives. He left the various officers to get on with the initial arrangements and was about to walk to the police station, when the young constable who had been guarding the front door came and found him.

"Please, sir, I have a message for you."

"Yes, officer, what is it?"

"There are several things, actually, sir, the skipper said I should tell you. First, the press are gathering in droves and are clamouring to know what is happening, and we are calling in reinforcements. Then we need to sort out what to do with the rest of the family, who are now bored with sitting upstairs and are demanding to see someone in charge. Then, the solicitor from over the road, a Mr Morrissey, came and spoke to me. He gave me his card, and says he thinks he might have some important information relating to a Major Greywell, that might be helpful to you. He says it might be quite urgent. Something to do with a will, I think he said. His office is over the bank, right across the street. He saw us putting out the tapes, and heard what had happened, and put two and two together. Seems a sensible sort of chap, says he'll wait in on your call. Any appointments he had have been cancelled, due to the weather."

"Thank you, officer. I don't know you, do I? Who are you?"

"PC Roger Cornwall, sir. I am the beat officer at Ingleton, just down the road. I'd come in to cover early turn here, because one of the other officers couldn't get in, he's snowed in up in the hills."

"You look frozen, I'll get someone to relieve you."

"Thank you, sir, I'm not too bad, as the lady here is plying us with coffee and biscuits. She just asked me to find out how you take yours."

"Did she? White, no sugar. What is this wonderful woman's name?"

"I only know her as Wendy. She's right shaken up, and she said she needed to do something. She also said she heard some movement in the pub last night. She sleeps in some nights."

"In which case, tell DI Allenby, please. Could you also tell her I'm going across the road to see this solicitor. The press will have to wait."

Saul walked across the road, into the chambers above the bank, told a rather bored looking secretary who he was, and waited in a reception area. He looked down at the front of the Golden Lion, and saw the press assembling. He mentally ran through the tasks to be done, and knew that by now most of the initial statements would be started. He saw the medical examiner leave the pub, and go down the road into the police station. He had known the woman for some years, and trusted her to tell him what she could, as soon as she could. There was no point in trying to get information before she was sure of her facts. They respected each other's professionalism. He saw the undertaker's vehicle arrive, and was wondering how they were going to move the body from the cupboard, when a soft voice said, "Superintendent Catchpole? I'm so sorry to keep you waiting, please come in. I think I can help you quite a lot. Would you like a coffee while you are here? Grace, would you bring some in, please?"

About an hour later, Saul left the office laden with copies of a variety of documents, and he was emerging into the street when a member of the press spotted him. He was instantly surrounded, and while he was being asked many questions, he held up his hand, and waited until there was silence.

"I will hold a press conference at the police station this afternoon. Shall we say four o'clock? Until then, you will get nothing, as I have nothing to tell you at this time. You know me well enough to accept that what I can tell you, I will. I suggest you find somewhere warm to go until then."

All but one of the reporters faded away. The one remaining was a nasty little man that Saul had disliked on sight two years before, and who was persistent to the point of rudeness, and they had crossed swords many times. Saul looked down at the man, and said, "I'm not giving you an exclusive, I will not answer any more questions, and I will not tolerate your attempts to hinder me or my team, in any way. Take this warning on board, Mr Andrews, because I mean it."

"Is it true that there are five bodies in there? I'll find out, there is only one way out, so they will have to come out onto the street at some time. I'm only doing my job. Come on, Mr Catchpole, I promise I'll only print what you want me to."

"I don't think so. Leave me alone, please, until I have something to tell you, and no, it isn't true."

He made it to the station, and was given an office. He made phone calls, and organised a press conference, and set various enquiries in motion. He called in the duty inspector, and asked, "Who was on duty last night? I need a complete log of any calls made or persons checked, or vehicles seen. I also need to speak to the officers who were on duty. Who were they?"

"Sergeant Graves, and Pc's Williams and Ord. They didn't get off until after seven, due to the weather, and one of the early turn not being able to make it in due to being snowed in up in the hills. He lives over at Malham, that is his designated beat. Shall I call those three in?"

"Not until they have had a decent amount of sleep. Ask them to come in after four, please. Incidentally, if my son comes in, would you ask him to take my car home? I'll get a lift back later. You'll know him, he has a shock of red hair, is about six foot two and looks very like me."

"You let your son drive your car? How brave of you."

"I know. He is an excellent driver, actually, better than I am. I'll leave the keys with you. What are we doing to feed all these troops we have called in? Please arrange for welfare to be organised. What is the weather forecast?"

"Snow, snow and more snow, accompanied by heavy frost in between. I hate to say it, but there is every chance we could be snowed in soon. Do you want me to see if there is somewhere you could stay?"

"Please, nothing too posh. There must be plenty of guest houses around. Find one for me, please, I'll ring my wife, and get her to pack a case for me. Bother this weather!"

He called into a café in the town square for a brief lunch, and then returned to the hotel. He was not surprised to find Andrews waiting with a camera right outside the pub. A quick conference with Celia established that Greywell's body had already been removed, and that the wall had been demolished under the stairs. The problem was how to remove the remaining two bodies to the mortuary.

"Take the whole settle, suitably wrapped, of course, in a van, and then take the other one. Have we got a time of death yet?"

"Not yet, no, but we have spoken to every one of the party and most of the staff. Greywell was a very hated man, not just by his relatives and staff, either. I had better update you with what we have so far. We have not spoken to the girl who found the bodies yet, but she seems to be an unlucky innocent, just a cleaner. She was given a sedative by her doctor and taken home. I'll get the statement from her, she should be awake by now."

"No, I want to see her myself. She is a great deal more involved than you imagine. I had a very interesting chat with the solicitor over the road. Have we had all the bodies identified yet, and next of kin informed?"

"Yes, and the coroner wishes to talk to you again."

"He lives here, doesn't he, in Giggleswick?"

"Yes. Here is his number."

"I'll ring him now."

Back at the Golden Lion, Saul went with Celia up to the staff flat. He could hear loud arguments as he made his way up the stairs. The experienced detective he had put in charge of them muttered, as he approached, "I'm sorry, guv, but I have tried to keep things reasonable. They are the most offensive, arrogant, bad tempered lot I have ever had to associate with. They have been accusing each other of all sorts, and now, I suspect they will be baying for your blood! Do you wish me to stay?"

"Please. Did you do as I ask, record what has been said by them all?"

"Yes, and they knew it, but it didn't seem to stop them. Good luck, guv!"

Saul walked into the sitting room and stood to the side of the settee, and waited. The outraged babblings finally ceased, and when there was an expectant hush, he said quietly, "Thank you for your patience, ladies and gentlemen. I am Detective Superintendent Catchpole, and I am in charge of this case. I am sorry you have been cooped up for so long, but in any case of murder, the forensic evidence we collect at the first opportunity is essential. To this purpose, as you are all under suspicion, your rooms and effects, including most of your vehicles, have been searched, and are now free for your re-occupation. Mr Greywell, your car, a blue Jaguar, has been recovered from a snow drift beside the road at Hellifield, and is now in the police station car park. You neglected to mention how it got there in your statement you made earlier, would you care to explain?"

"I trust you have warrants to search our rooms and belongings?"

"No, Mr Windle, I do not. The whole building is a crime scene, and has been treated as such. I do not need a warrant in these circumstances, as you should be well aware."

"Are you arresting anyone?"

"Not at the moment, but I will if I have to. You have all made statements. Some of the things you have said I already know to be inaccurate. Others are not true, and other matters which are very relevant have been omitted. Please return to your rooms, or meet downstairs. If anyone wishes to amend their statements, my officers will be in the dining room. Three of your party have already been murdered. Initially the evidence suggests that someone from your party is either a killer or at least involved. I would be very careful, and trust no one. Mr Greywell, I await your explanation. If anyone desires to leave the building, I ask you inform one of my officers."

"We are free to go?"

"You are; but I will wish to talk to all of you, so if you chose to stay here, it might help."

"And if we do go?"

"I will visit you where ever you are. Before you make a mass exodus, I will inform you that most of the roads are blocked, and the trains delayed, probably cancelled. I doubt you will get far, at least tonight."

"In other words we are stuck here?"

"It looks like it, yes. This is a comfortable hotel. I have spoken to the owner, your accommodation is paid for, and so I ask you to stop here until we have got a little further with our investigations. Those of you who are innocent will, hopefully, assist me."

"And those of us who won't, will be suspected, innocent or not!"

"You said it, Mr Windle; if that is how you wish to interpret it, carry on."

"How dare you treat us like this? I'm going to complain about you. First you imprison us up here, then you search our rooms, accuse us of lying, and generally suggest we are all liars, murderers and fugitives from justice."

Celia and the two detectives in the room winced. They knew that Catchpole was an easy going boss, quiet, firm and very fair, but all of them had glimpsed, on the odd occasion, his underlying temper, when pushed too far. He was not a man you wished to provoke, and was treated with great respect by his fellow officers.

"Mrs Arbuthnot, I dare because it is my job. By all means complain. It will not alter the way I act. I am sorry that you have lost your brother, and make allowances for your very well concealed grief over the matter. That goes all for all of you, but make no mistake, I will find who killed all three men, and bring them to justice. It is actually what I am very good at, which is why I'm in charge. I'm not paid to be nice, kind, stupid or bullied. I will do it with or without your cooperation, so any futile attempts to obstruct me will only serve to make your lives a lot harder, and believe me, I can do that. If you won't talk to me here, we can arrange for it to be done at the police station, and you can stay in a cell if you like. Do I make myself understood?"

Julia Arbuthnot sat down, and everybody went very quiet. One by one they went downstairs, leaving Saul and Greville Greywell in the room.

"I'm still waiting to know why your car was taken out some time last night."

"I couldn't stand the atmosphere in here last night. Cecil was pontificating at length, in the Writing Room, about how useless we all were, and I needed to get out for some air. I took it out about eleven, and got two villages down, and it got stuck in that ditch. I thought I was in for a cold walk back, but this man stopped and gave me a lift. He was driving one of those big quarry lorries. Gerry, I think he said his name was. He dropped me off at the roundabout on the bypass. I got in about one, let myself in the back door and went straight up to bed."

"Then why not mention it to my officer when you made your statement?"

"I didn't want my wife to know I'd been driving. Look, I'll be straight with you, I'd had a few drinks, and she will be livid with me. I was probably over the limit. That's why."

"Thank you, please don't waste my time or that of my officers, by not mentioning things again. Lying to the police can be a serious business, as you well know."

"What do you mean?"

"I mean I know just who you are, and your convictions and involvement in handling stolen goods, so don't treat any of us as though you were an innocent. I'm not a fool, Mr Greywell. I'll talk to you later."

Saul went straight to the police station, where he gave the basic facts to the press, and then headed for his office. Samuel was waiting outside the office.

"You still here? I thought I'd sent you home, did you not get my message? Your mother will need the car."

"Yes, I did. It's OK, Dad, I've been home, packed a bag for you, and brought it back by train. I told her what the score was. The roads are mostly blocked."

"So how are you going to get home?"

"I'm not, I don't think. Not tonight anyway, so I asked the inspector here where you were stopping, and I got a room for the night at the same place. I've just about got enough money left to pay for it."

"All right, fair enough. This wouldn't have anything to do with Ruth's imminent arrival, I suppose?"

"Yes, sorry Dad, but I can't stand her. I got those presents, and hid them in my room. I know, you won't have time for me, I'll do my own thing. There are other pubs here you know, unless there is anything I can do to help."

"Where are we staying?"

"The bed and breakfast next to the railway station. It's very nice, nice people, and the food is great. They have already given me something to eat. They only have the two rooms, so it will just be you and me tonight. I know, you'll be back really late."

"Too right. Look Sam, just be a bit careful, will you? Yes, I would quite like to hear any gossip, anything you can listen to, but remember, someone has already killed. Here, take a little spending money, and find out what you can. Don't talk to any journalist or reporters, please, but I would like to know what is being said."

Saul was reading through some of the statements that had been taken, when he received a call from the pathologist. He made notes, and then called a meeting of all his detective team, and some of the local officers, in the parade room at the police station.

"I have had an initial report from the pathologist, she is doing the full PMs tomorrow morning. Greywell was killed last night, or more accurately between one thirty and three this morning. The body in the settle has been dead some days, but died about twenty-four hours before the one in the cupboard. DI Allenby is collating all of this. Until we have all the facts, it is best not to jump to conclusions. I had a long talk to the solicitor over the road, and Greywell almost expected something like this. He called the meeting of his family and dependents, here, to complete certain tasks he needed to do. He was less than honest with them; he knew that one way or another, he had not long to live. Maybe a year or two at the most. His heart was failing. He was well aware that some of them could be pushed to kill, if necessary, to protect themselves. Before he arrived here, he prepared various letters, about every single one of his family, so the truth would be known. These letters were held at his house in York, and he told the solicitor chap here where they could be found.

"This morning, I got through to York, and arranged for these documents to be obtained. He had listed all the letters. I have the faxes of most of them, but several are missing. The only way anyone could get into his safe, without blowing it apart, which had not happened, was to collect the keys, one of only two sets, from his solicitor in York. This we did. The only other set was here, with him, and they are still in his pocket. I got the pathologist to check. Somehow, someone must have borrowed the keys, either taken copies of them and had another set made, or used the original set, to get into his house, open the safe and remove the letters relevant to some of those listed."

"Why are these documents so important, sir?"

"Because, Sergeant, they included a complete history of almost all his associates, employees, and also a detailed account, almost a confession, of his own misdeeds, including the people who he had, as he puts it, bested in his career. I haven't read all of it yet, but what I have read is dynamite! So far as I can see, it gives every one of his party, and a lot of locals, a sound motive for murder. By tomorrow, I shall have read it all, and the statements we have so far, and we will have copies for all the office managers, supervisors and investigating officers. These must not be left out, and must be secured in the station safe when not in your possession. Celia, as we are now snowed in, has everyone got accommodation and all they need?"

"Yes, just, sir. The press have taken over several guest houses, but I managed to get everyone a bed, except the local officers."

"Good. Now, any questions?"

"What time do you want us to start in the morning?"

"I shall be in early, I expect you in by eight, unless I or DI Allenby say otherwise. Celia, please brief the supervisors, while I talk to the nights crew from last night. We can busy ourselves this evening. There are plenty of avenues to explore."

"Do you need anyone to mix with the locals, see what the talk is?"

"Once your designated tasks are completed, by all means, but I already have someone doing that. I don't need to remind you not to talk to the press, at all, and there will be no drinking expenses tonight!"

In his office, Saul spoke to Pc's Ord and Williams. One had been in the custody suite at Skipton from ten thirty until four, and the other had been dealing with an accident at Clapham on the A 65 from eleven until one, and then was sent directly to a stranded coach at Ingleton, and from there to Horton in Ribblesdale to deal with the sudden death of an old lady there, and had not returned to Settle until six thirty. He asked for a copy of their pocket note books, and that they write out detailed statements for the night. He asked them to mention anything unusual that they remembered, and sent them off to write their statements.

He called Adrian Graves in next, and sat him down. Before he could say anything, Adrian said, "Sir, I think I should tell you, you may wish to treat me as a suspect. Not only did I have quite a bit of contact with Major Greywell, I had every reason to intensely dislike him on personal grounds. He was the reason my father had to leave the Force, many years ago. I am delighted he is dead, but I didn't actually kill him. I have tried to be fair and unprejudiced in my dealings with him, and will help you all I can. I was out and about last night, and here is my pocket book, which is accurate, and was made up at the time. While I have been waiting, I have jotted down some recollections of the evening, that were not at the time worthy of noting."

"How refreshingly frank of you! Yes, he mentions a Graves in his memoirs, I hadn't connected it. You are local, born and bred here. I will be grateful of your help, but as you are aware, I cannot discount anyone. I will not, therefore, be including you in the investigation team, but I may need your input on local matters. Are you very offended?"

"No, not at all. I'm rather relieved. I won't ask, but I will tell you what I know. Is that acceptable?"

"Quite. Are you on duty tonight?"

"Yes, sir, for the rest of the week. I take it you want me to run the rest of the station, and leave the others to assist you?"

"I think you and I are going to get on very well. Under normal circumstances, I would move you to another station until I can eliminate you, but the weather has dictated we will need any officer we can get. Have we anyone else we can call on?"

"We have three special constables, all reliable, living in the town, and an officer on leave, but I think she has gone home to her family in Cumbria, I'll check. Shall I confer with DI Allenby about them?"

"If you would. I would like a foot patrol in the centre of town through the night, if possible. Not you, but some other officers."

"Leave that to me sir. I take it you would like a statement of all I know, including hearsay and circumstantial evidence?"

"I would. As soon as you can please."

The murder squad room was busy, and the computers being set up, when Saul went to find Celia. Over a cup of coffee in the kitchen, he said, "I leave it to you, Celia, to organise the tasks and welfare, and the actions for each officer. I have copied everything I have so far, and there are copies for you, but please, ensure they are secure. Could you organise a file on every suspect, as well as all witnesses? You don't need me to tell you. So far, apart from the weather, have we any unexpected problems?"

"Nothing I cannot handle, sir. Do you want me to read it all tonight?"

"Heavens, no! I will try, but you are going to be far too busy. Tomorrow, or the next day maybe, they all need to be read, by several of us to ensure we don't miss anything. We have worked together often enough to know what each of us is good at, but may I make a suggestion?"

"Of course."

"Although we cannot rule anyone out, I suspect that the happy family gathering in the Golden Lion holds at least one killer. They may not have finished their little murder spree yet, and I think you should consider having an officer awake and patrolling the pub all night, or at least monitoring the comings and goings. Only the staff and the party will be there tonight, we should be able to open the bars up for trade after it is cleaned tomorrow. The owner is being ever so cooperative, but he does need his business back, this will hit him hard enough as it is. It is just possible that someone might just want to talk to the officer without any of the others knowing."

"If you think it is necessary, yes. We are rather struck for manpower, I'll see what I can do. We will all be there until quite late. I could sit in there myself, and do some paperwork, with a sort of 'I'm available if you want to tell me something' look on my face."

"Good idea, but I wouldn't drink anything I wasn't sure of, not from that bar, or take anything from any of the party. I also want to know who goes out, who with, and when they return. Don't leave a poor Pc in the snow and cold all night, I have the outside covered."

"How do we stop unwanted callers?"

"Celia, really! Just lock the front doors, and allow access only by the back door. There is a bell, I checked."

"Oh, yes, how silly of me. I'll get on. Where will you be during the evening?"

"Here, probably, if not, on my mobile. You know where I am staying? Good, if anything happens, please, if you need me, ring. I may pop in and talk a few things through with you during the evening. I would think it was a good idea to have two on in the pub, but that is up to you."

Chapter Eight

Ruby was very angry with Greville. The whole week was turning into a disaster. She was not getting the normal amount of attention she expected. Things were getting rather dangerous. She had no intention of paying Cecil or Greville anything for her jewellery. Apart from a steady and unlimited supply of gin, it was the most precious thing in her life. Greville had long before ceased to pay her any attention, and she was missing the clandestine meetings with her lover. She had parted from some of her jewellery, to give to him, and was worried that Greville might find out. She need no longer fear Cecil, but she couldn't afford anyone looking too closely into her affairs, either of the heart, or anything else. Greville had asked some very awkward questions recently. She had listened to what everyone had said while they were in the flat upstairs. Something was worrying her, something someone had said, or she had seen the previous evening. That several of the party had not told the truth to the police, was obvious. She did not believe her dear husband had felt the need to escape the atmosphere the night before, nor had he been that drunk. He had gone to either meet someone, or to get something. She knew he had been talking to Windle during the last couple of days rather a lot. Windle was a quite frequent visitor at their home in London. Greville said he was advising him, but there was more to it than that.

Ruby put on her flashiest jewellery, and went down to the pool room and ordered a large gin and tonic from Tim, the barman. Greville had warned her not to wear the intricate, very heavy and, she knew, valuable crucifix, in public. In this remote area, she couldn't expect anyone to know what it was, or even what it was worth. She had also worn a quite exquisite and intricate brooch, and the earrings from the same set, because it made her feel better, and it would annoy Greville intensely.

She sat in the corner of the pool room, and soon she was joined by her daughters. Melanie said, "I'm going to spend the evening in one of the other pubs. I can't stand it in here. That creep Oliver Windle thinks if he is nice enough to me he'll get lucky, and so does Bill. There is much better company elsewhere. I trust you don't think we should mourn Uncle Cecil, because I never could stand him. I won't pretend now. I never intended to pay him for the flat. After the way he used to touch me up, it was the least he could do."

"You never told me that. No, you go where you want. Are you going, Samantha?"

"Yes, I am. No doubt the pigs will want to know where we are, but they can go to hell. I think I could do with a drink, out of here."

"Don't be too late coming in. Do you need any money?"

"No, I found some earlier. I need to get it changed, so I'll get some fags at the Spar shop, and I'll grab a bite while I'm out."

"Where on earth did you find money? You were skint yesterday?"

"Never mind, but if it is left lying around, then I'm going to liberate it. Uncle Cecil gave me some yesterday, I asked him for it. He wanted to be left alone to talk to someone, not sure who, but I cottoned on that if I hung around, then he might pay me to go away. It was quite late, and I think he was a bit embarrassed I was still around. Miles went to see him, but left, and then Oliver, which is when he gave me the money. See you folks later. Do you want another drink in that, Mum, before I go?"

"Yes, please. Sam, did Cecil ever abuse you, sexually, I mean?"

"Sure he did. I told Dad, and it stopped. I tried to tell you, but you wouldn't listen. I got out of Uncle Cecil's way whenever I could. That's why he never said anything when I took things from him sometimes. I expect he thought it was so long ago I'd forgotten it, when he asked me for some things back. Well, he's not getting them now, for sure! I sold most of them. I got a lot of money from that silly icon thing he got when he was in Italy. He said he didn't like it much, so I sold it down the Portobello Road. I had to get rid of it cheaper than it was worth, because the first dealer I took it to said he thought it was a listed stolen piece of art from just after the war. Taken from Carrara, or something like that, where the marble comes from, so he said, together with loads of priceless jewellery that was the property of some family or religious order. I know Uncle Cecil said he had brought the picture thing back from Italy, when he was in the army. He was posted there, he said, as an interpreter for some bridge project, I know he told me it was over a river called the Po, I remember that because I thought it funny."

Samantha brought over a large drink, already mixed with tonic, before going up to Celia, who was sitting in the dining room, and saying, "Me and my sister are going out for the evening. We will visit one of the other pubs. We'll be back later."

"Thank you for telling me. Please leave and return by the back door. Do you have a key?"

"On our key rings."

Saul took off his reading glasses, sat back in his chair and stretched his long legs. He looked up at the Special Constable who had come in, and accepted a mug of coffee from him.

"Well thank you! How long are you on for?"

"Until there is nothing more for me to do. I'm self employed, and was taking a break until after Christmas. Sergeant Graves asked me to stay in the station and run it, you know, the normal tasks, to release a regular officer. He has to stay in, as we have two drunks in the cells. If you need anything, please just shout for me. Everyone calls me Mo. Mo Tasker. I'm pleased I can help. I've been here for years, have to retire next year, I shall miss it."

"What is Mo short for?"

"It's a bit silly, my mother was a Sherlock Holmes fan, my brother was called Sherlock, and my elder brother was called Mycroft. I got lumbered with Moriarty! I don't want to seem presumptuous, but if you need directions or local knowledge, I know most everyone round here, and probably their parents and distant cousins as well. One of the few advantages of being incredibly old!"

"I wish you could come on the team for a day or two, until we have got straight. I don't want to wreck your family life, but I will accept your offer of help."

"I don't really have a family. My wife passed on six years ago, and all my children have moved away, two abroad in Australia, and one in the navy. I wouldn't be a nuisance, but I'd love it. My time is really my own. I've never been involved in anything so exciting, I'm quite happy to do the menial stuff, to give a real officer more time to do their job."

"This enquiry could last a while, are you sure?"

"It'd be the most exciting Christmas I've had for years. Give me something to do, rather than watching a load of repeats on the box."

"Then welcome to the team, Mo. Yes, I can use you. First, could you find me some plain file covers, some plastic sleeves, a wad of plain paper or an exercise book, several of them? I don't suppose there is such a thing as a bottle of black ink around? Also, we need some highlighters, a white board and writers. Are you au fait with the copier here? It completely mystified me."

"Yes, we are old adversaries. I know it better than most, I service the thing. That's my line of work. If these things are not available in the station, do you want me to go out and get them? The newsagent will still be open, if he isn't, I know him, and he'll open up for me."

"Thanks, here, take this money, and get a receipt."

"Will you be wanting blotting paper? They do red ink, if you need it, as well as blue and black."

"Yes to all of those. Do you mind being my gopher?"

"Not at all. I'll go now. I'll just check with Mr Graves, and then come straight back. Need anything else, smokes, chewing gum, mints, headache pills?"

"You do think ahead. No to the smokes, yes to the mints and yes to the headache pills, please. Is there enough money there?"

"Plenty, sir."

Celia came in, and began to file papers and organise the work scheduled for the following day. She saw Oliver Windle come down and go into the pool room, and sit beside Ruby. Soon the rest of the group followed him. They were watching something on the wide screen television. Miles and Alana were huddled together round the fire. Wilfred was talking to Ted and Percy, and Greville was talking to Colin Darbury, and was joined by Bill. Julia was sitting alone. Tim was behind the bar, and there was a gentle murmur of conversation, none of which seemed very interesting to Celia. Oliver Windle went upstairs, and Julia moved over and talked to Ruby. The flow of drinks to the whole party seemed steady. Tim collected glasses from time to time.

They all collected in the dining room, and sat down for supper. The Italian head waiter, Giuseppe, was serving them, when he stopped suddenly, and stared at Ruby. Celia watched with interest, as he recovered himself.

Several times he paused, during the meal, and looked at her. He spoke softly to her, at the end of the meal, asking her something about the jewellery she was wearing. Celia wasn't really paying attention, but after the party had returned to the pool room, he was agitated, so she asked him, "What's the matter? What has upset you? It is something to do with what Mrs Greywell is wearing?"

"It is a' nothing. The cross and brooch she wear, it is like something I have seen before. From when I was a child in Italy. It is worth a lot of money, I think. It should not be on a woman like that. It must be a copy. I must help Paul in the kitchen."

Giuseppe went off muttering to himself. That he was upset was obvious. As Giuseppe had not been on duty during the period of the other murders, Celia was unconcerned. She was surprised when Miles and Colin came to her and Miles said, "The waiter was rather upset. He wanted to know where she had got that flashy cross and jewellery. She said Major Greywell gave it to her. That isn't actually true. It was in the stock of his brother's jewellery business. We had it on the inventory, checked it last year, didn't we, Colin?"

"Yes, he said it was too valuable to be used. He did lend some items to his brother for some sort of display in the shop, so I suppose that's how she got it. I also know it was mentioned in his will specifically, and it was to be left to someone else, Alana, I believe. Definitely not Ruby. Major Greywell hated her."

"Thank you, I'll check it out."

Celia did not attach much importance to the matter. It seemed very trivial. She needed to make a number of calls, and as it was obvious that no one was going to volunteer any information, she went to the office by the back door, and worked there. A local Pc, Pc Ord came and checked in with her, and he remained there while she went over to the police station. At eleven, she returned and dismissed him, telling him to cover the external foot patrol of the town centre.

Melanie and Samantha came in at about half past ten, and went up to their room. Celia watched Ted, Percy and Wilfred go to their rooms at the same time. Celia was in the corridor when Julia entered her room, and Alana disappeared to her room at the end of the back corridor. Miles and Colin went to their room and Bill went to his next door.

Celia Allenby was ambitious. She wanted her own command, and rather resented any form of supervision. She had often worked with Saul Catchpole, and found him a little old-fashioned, and meticulous in his ways. He was always polite, considerate of his staff, and listened to any opinions, including hers, but almost invariably did what he was going to have done in the first place. He double-checked everything that was done, not just by her, but all the supervisors, and she felt he was a little out of touch with modern methods. He was known for erring on the side of caution. She considered that he wasted time, and a lot of money, and was afraid to channel enquiries into the most productive avenues. She rather resented his quiet assumption of control. He was remarkably successful, and to be associated with him was good for her career, but she hoped when he was made up to Chief Superintendent, in the New Year, she would be given more autonomy. As she sat waiting, she considered that she would handle things a bit differently when she was in charge. She was tired, and it was a fair walk back to her guest house.

Back in the bar, Ruby was sat at her table with a selection of gin and tonics in front of her. Oliver Windle got up, and left Greville and Ted talking to Ruby. There was a hushed argument between Greville and Ruby, and Ted wished Tim and Celia a cheery goodnight, and she saw him head up to his room. Greville was going into his room as she checked the corridors.

Down in the bar, Tim was clearing up. Celia watched as he asked Ruby if she wanted him to clear the glasses in front of her. She said, "No, leave them. I want to sit quietly here for a while. You close the bar, and get off home, dearie."

Tim cleared up around her, and as he was about to leave, she said, "Give us another one, then I'll be off to bed soon."

Tim did so, and then checked Celia had all she needed. They discussed who on the staff was sleeping in, and she found out that Giuseppe was sleeping in Wendy's room overnight. The kitchen staff had gone home. Apart from Ruby, the bars were deserted. Celia did another tour of the upstairs corridors, and heard several snores, and some televisions on. She came down, and spoke to Ruby.

"Are you heading upstairs soon?"

"In a bit. I'm just very tired, and I have some thinking to do. You push off, love. I'll be fine."

Celia noticed that her speech was slurred, and she was very drunk. Celia thought about pulling in an officer to watch the pub, but decided that the whole idea was a waste of time and money.

She packed up her things, and left by the back door. At the police station, she left a note for the early turn to check the pub, and left a key in an envelope.

She passed Pc Ord in the Market Square, on her way to her guest house. It had stopped snowing, but there was a heavy frost. She was soon tucked up in bed.

At the police station, coffee and biscuits arrived hourly for the rest of the evening. Saul wandered down to the cell block, and found Adrian Graves busily writing.

"Just finishing that statement and notes, sir. Can I get you something?"

"No, thank you. Is Mo for real? He seems an absolute gem."

"He is. He is more use than a handful of probationers. He is the best example of 'big ears and a little mouth' I know. He says you have some work for him, and he is flattered you can use him. Shall I write him off to help you?"

"Yes, please. You run a tight ship here, Graves. This is about the tidiest station I've visited. How do I get in, if the station is closed?"

"I'll issue you a key to your office, the only one, and programme you in to the keypad lock on the back door. I'll be around all night, I'm afraid, these drunks won't be sober until the morning."

Saul returned to his office; Mo arrived with his supplies, and was quietly leaving, when Saul said, "Mo, just a minute. Do you know a Jack and Jo Atterthwaite?"

"I do, and their father. He's in a wheelchair after a stroke years ago. They live out on a smallish farm, about three miles away. Do you want me to show you on the map? I got one out of the cupboard for you?"

Having established several locations, Saul paused and said, "How about Archie Babble? Where does he live?"

"Here, in town. I've got you a street map, I'll show you. I certainly know Archie. Bit of a character. From what I hear, he threatened this Greywell chap the other night and tried to strangle him. If it's true, then he would have been drunk. He's a loud mouthed, bolshie drunk, and a timid, retiring lad when he is sober. His bark is usually worse than his bite, but when he's had a skinful he can be violent. Not the most brilliant mind, I must admit, but he is an excellent mechanic when he wants to be. He'll be out with the council gritting tonight, I expect."

"Would he have been out last night?"

"He was. He lives just up from me, and I saw him come in about a quarter to two in the morning."

"Did you know Sergeant Graves' father? He was an inspector here years ago."

"Not well. I joined the Specials a bit after he left. He lives up at Kirkby Lonsdale now. I've heard a bit about this Greywell chap, over the years. He's been the talk of the town the last few days. There is a lot of bad feeling about what he did when he was here, a bit before my time in the Force. I know he ruined a lot of gullible men, and their families. Not sure how, exactly. I believe two men topped themselves because of it. There was inquests into them, I know that. One shot himself with his shotgun, the other hanged himself in his barn. His daughter works at the pub now. She would have been five, six, when it happened. Her mother married again. Nice lass, Wendy is her name. Then there was the talk about the lassie, Brenda. There was some scandal about her mother and Greywell, some allegation by her against him, but I never knew much more. She

105

is now married to our local dentist, Tim Royce. There must be records of it all, shall I look them out for you?"

"I doubt it, it is about twenty-five years ago. They must have been destroyed long ago, or put onto computer. Pity, it could have been helpful."

"No, the records were not destroyed. I know where they are. They should have been, but they got missed, for some reason. If I remember right, they were meant to go to HQ for destruction, but there was a fire, and they never got collected. They are down in the basement, rooms of them. No one goes down there. I knows we shouldn't have them, but we do. I don't think there is anyone but me knows they are down there. Everyone thinks the key to them rooms was lost, but I know where it is. Found it not long ago, when I was clearing out the old stable block. I just put it on the key board, and no one has asked about it. Do you want me to go and find them, it could take a while?"

"Yes, please, see if you can locate them, but could I ask you to hang fire, I'll give you a list of incidents and names to research. They will all be within a three-year period I think. I'll have it for you tomorrow. Could you do it then?"

"I'll start in the morning. Best not to mention this to anyone else, I expect. No one will think anything of it, I'm sort of unofficial handyman here anyway, fix the odd thing, gives me something to do. I gets paid for it, a bit. They also use me as a civilian gaoler, and I do a bit of part time civilian driver as well. No call for a full-time one here."

"You are authorised to drive police vehicles?"

"Yes. Everything we have here, anyway, not traffic cars and bikes, but everything else. I do correspondence runs to HQ and Skipton, and drive the prison van, things like that."

"Mo, you are a gem. The answer to many of my problems. Were you wafted here from paradise?"

"No, nor Luton Airport, neither. If it's all right with you, sir, I'll make another cuppa for everyone, and then go and see if I can find if them files is in chronological order."

Chapter Nine

Saul's eyes were starting to go fuzzy. He had made copious notes, and read almost all the available information. He found Mo, and told him he was going to his lodgings to get some sleep. He signed out, informed the Control Room of his movements, picked up his briefcase and mobile phone, and went out of the front door as Mo, with a civilian jacket on, joined him on the steps.

It dawned on Saul he had no idea where his lodgings were. The snow was deep, and there was a howling blizzard. He looked around for some inspiration. He turned to Mo.

"I don't suppose you know where I'm meant to be staying?"

"To be sure I do. You are at the Station Guest House. I'm going that way, I'll walk down there with you, it isn't far. I live a little further on. Nice couple, Chris and his wife. He's the local decorator."

Mo walked Saul to the door of the guest house, and wished him a cheery good night as he disappeared into the blizzard. Sam was watching for him, and let him in. It was very late, and he said softly, "They left a meal for you in the kitchen, and showed me how to use the microwave. I'll heat it up for you. I unpacked your bag, Dad, I'll show you your room. You have a bathroom en suite. I expect you want to get your head down. They left a breakfast for you, 'cos I thought you'd be out early. If you don't want it, I'll eat it, and mine. She is a brilliant cook! Then I'll let you get to bed. I've had quite an evening. Found out quite a lot, but it will wait until morning. I've written it all down for you."

"Well done, Sam. I'll not be sleeping for a bit, sit and share this meal with me, I'll never eat all that!"

"I was hoping you would say that. Mum reckons I've got worms or something. Dad, I need to talk to you, not now, necessarily, but soon. Are you too tired?"

"Is this going to be an epic discussion on the meaning of life, or the origin of the universe? If so, the answer is yes, I am. If it is a short confession to some awful transgression, yes, but anything else, no. Is something worrying you?"

"In a way, yes. Look, I've been doing a lot of thinking recently, about what I want to do."

"I thought you wanted to do sports science at university?"

"Well, I don't, not any more. Haven't done for a while. Yes, I love sport, but when it is more like work than fun, the sparkle, and the kick of it sort of goes down the plughole. Sure, I want to train, but I want to do something else."

"Then choose another course at university. You got good enough grades to do what you want."

"I don't want to go to university either. I've been finding out a lot, about all sorts of things. I don't want the armed forces, or computers and that. I want to join the Police."

"You do, whatever for?"

"I'd like to get as far as you have. It is interesting, and I think I can do it. I know it is not all a bed of roses, the hours are long, but I'd like to try it."

"Is this because of me? If it is, my being a copper should have no influence on your decision. I'm very flattered, and rather pleased, but I had hoped you would do something better with your life. I would rather you got a degree first, Sam. It gives you so many options, and when you have one, then you can do whatever takes your fancy, with my whole-hearted blessing."

"I rather thought that is what you would say, so I will think about it. So long as you know that is what I want to do. Would you object to my becoming a Special for a while, until then?"

"Good move. You have thought this through, I can see that, but please, if you wish to impress me, get a good degree first."

"I thought you weren't keen on Specials?"

"Yes, and no. I met one today, who is a splendid example of how they can help the regular force. It is the system that allows them I don't approve of, not the men and women themselves, who give up their time to help the community. I only see one major problem with your plan."

"What?"

"Your mother, how she will react, not to mention Ruth!"

"Mum will do her crust, won't she?"

"Yes, how were you planning to handle that?"

Sam looked at his father with dismay. "Well, I sort of wondered, I mean, well, perhaps?"

"So your plan was to get me to suggest it, and be in the dog-house, so that eventually she would come round, and if it all goes wrong it will be my fault! Thank you, son, for your kind thoughts."

"Could you not sort of suggest it, to make me realise it would be a seriously wrong turn to take, so I would come out of this 'silly' phase, as Auntie Ruth puts it? Then when it is an accepted fact, I could announce that I liked it, and they couldn't make such a thing of it?"

"You devious bugger! I hate to admit this, but you might be an excellent copper, after all. Just how long have you been hatching all this up?"

"About three months. Dad, would you really be in the poo with Mum?"

"Yes. She can hardly wait for me to retire. She and Ruth, and I suspect the girls, have jobs lining up for when I can no longer escape and will be imprisoned in the house. I have no intention of retiring until they push me out with my Zimmer frame. I love your mother very much, but there are limits, Sam. My advice to you is to get out as soon as you can. Stephen never came back to live after he first went to university. His living on the Isle of Man rather inhibits the female side of the family descending on him. Have you discussed this with him?"

"My dear elder brother, yes, Dad, I have, last week when I was over there. He suggested asking you to tackle Mum over it. He sends his fondest love, by the way, and wants to know when you are going over for some male bonding. He said he and Mum fell out when he moved away from home, and you got the flack, and he's sorry, but he's not coming back."

"Did I! I should say! I'm not sorry, for all I got earache for ages, because I needed him to escape. He needed to. The trouble with matriarchal women like Ruth, and to some extent your mother, is that they cannot conceive of any man being able to run their lives without their interference. Had Ruth not been such a forceful character, and brought your mother up when their parents died, Diana might be able to resist her interference. Just when I think things are relaxing, and we are getting on fine, Ruth descends again. I tried so hard when we first married to tell her to butt out, but I nearly lost your mother over it. If I had asked her to choose between Ruth and marriage, I might just have lost. I'm quite amazed that neither you or Stephen are gay."

"Well, that's the other thing…"

"Are you?"

"No, not at all, neither is Stephen, just kidding, Dad! You should have see your face! No, definitely not, but I shy away from bossy women like mad. I am so glad I didn't go to Auntie Ruth's school, or the one Mum teaches at, either."

"I made sure of that. I said if they insisted, I would move to another area to prevent it. They told me I was wrecking your chance of a good education, but I don't consider you did so bad. I'm glad the girls don't get taught by either of them, they would get hell if the other kids knew, I think!"

"Sharon is just as bossy as Aunt Ruth, but Susan is all right."

"Yes, I know. I've taken steps to sort that out. OK, Sam, I'll help you, because a major row is brewing anyway, so we might just make it worthwhile, and kill two birds with one stone. I've decided that both your sisters will be better at a different school. Sharon is becoming a very spoilt little madam, and her marks are disgraceful. Susan is being bullied, by Sharon and the others in her set, and I had a long talk with both of them last week. Your mother won't believe it, and says that she will have to ask Ruth about it, but I won't have it. I am going to make a stand on this, and I told Diana so."

"So this case has been rather opportune, you getting away for a few days?"

"Very."

"Dad, when Mum chucks you out, can I come and live with you?"

"Yes. It may come to that, I hope it won't. Ruth's visits are becoming more frequent, and more unbearable. I will not see the girls ruined because she is incapable of having her own relationship. I suppose you had better know, I told Diana this is the last Christmas Ruth comes, and after this, she will not stay unless I agree. She doesn't believe I mean it, but I can be remarkably stubborn, if I need to be."

"Why did I have to take your car back to Mum? She has her own one. Why couldn't she use hers?"

"Because Ruth prefers mine, it is more comfortable. I offered your mother one like mine, but she says it is too expensive for her to run. The fact that I cannot fit into the mini, not except in an emergency, means that I cannot swap. All is not well between your mother and me, Sam. I don't want to make her choose, but I think I shall have to."

"I'm sorry, Dad. Can I help?"

"Yes, you can. Don't wimp out on me. Our problems must not affect your life choices. I love you, all you kids, very much, and it is only for the sake of peace and quiet that I have not made a stand before, but Ruth was never as bad before. Since her last partner ran out on her, she has latched onto Diana, and it is suffocating us. Your mother's attitude towards you, and to some extent the girls, has changed over the last six months. She has been pretty nasty to you, I think, why didn't you tell me?"

"Because I could see how horrid she was being to you, I didn't want to make things worse. I'm old enough to look after myself."

"So that's why you want to get a job, to get away?"

"Partly. She said I should be doing more to help around the house, as you were never there. She didn't like it at all when you gave me that motorbike when I passed my test, and I didn't have to rely on her to give me lifts to college. She expects me home as soon as college finishes, and wants to know where I am all the time."

"Yes, this controlling thing is becoming an obsession. I won't have it. I'll tell you something, Sam. Ages ago, I bought a flat just outside town. I've had it done up. I was going to rent it out if I didn't need it. You are welcome to move in there, I know you can be sensible. I was hoping to sleep there when I'm very busy on a case. It has two bedrooms. Move in there in the New Year, if you want to. I probably shan't be far behind you, unless I can deal with Ruth."

"I do love you, Dad. Are you very unhappy?"

"Pretty much, yes. I love you, but now, I must get some sleep. Fancy staying here with me until we have resolved this case? What will you do tomorrow, or today as it is now?"

"Whatever I can to help you, then do a bit of winter walking, then sit in the pubs and listen. See you later, Dad. I'm sorry I've kept you up."

"I'm not, I need to know how you really feel. You may be grown up, but that is what fathers are for, you know. Good night."

Chapter Ten

Saul woke early and gratefully ate some of the breakfast left for him and drank two cups of coffee, before walking over to the police station. Sgt Graves was still on duty, and Pc Ord came in covered in snow, as Saul went up to the office he had been loaned.

He took the documents from the safe, and finished reading the last of them. It was still early in the morning, and he walked over to the Golden Lion and was surprised when he could get no reply from the bell and the place was still in darkness. He pulled a set of keys from his pocket, and let himself in. He found the light switches in the main bar and switched all the lights on, and went upstairs and checked the corridors, expecting to find a patrolling officer on watch. When he could find no one, he rang the station and spoke to Adrian Graves.

"Skipper, who was supposed to be on duty in the pub last night?"

"DI Allenby said she had it covered. I offered her two officers, but she said they were not necessary, and she covered it herself until about midnight. She said if she needed someone she would get them from the CID. Is that where you are?"

"Yes. I'll stay here until someone turns up. Could you leave her a message to ring me when she comes in, if I am not back by then?"

"Sure, look, I can let you have WPc Barber now, if you like. She has just come on duty. She is a probationer, rather new, but a sensible lass. I'll send her over. Is everything all right, do you need assistance?"

"No, I'm fine. I hope everything is all right. Yes, please send her over. There should be staff coming in soon."

Saul was furious. He was not accustomed to having his suggestions ignored. He admitted to himself that he found working with Celia very frustrating. She was always very self-confident, and he was aware that she found his approach and methods very old-fashioned at times, and would often try to implement her new ideas, but he tried to accept that there was often more than one way to do things. He had consciously tried to give her areas of responsibility in which she could exercise her authority. Often she would do it in a way he would have avoided. He tried very hard to consider his staff and their welfare, and if her career was to progress, she had to make some of her own decisions. On several occasions she had tried to upstage him, by dazzling their seniors with her brilliant new ideas and methods, but she was clever enough to mask her intentions, by expressing how valuable working with him could be, how she was learning so much from him and his considerable experience. He accepted that he was old-fashioned, and that was how he got the results he did. He had tried so hard with her, and had learned that giving orders to her was often counter-productive, and had found that suggesting methods of working was much better. That she resented him and sought to replace him was obvious. She made the mistake of making it obvious that she considered him an old fuddy-duddy at times. He decided to see what the repercussions were, before making a point of it. It was hardly likely that any great harm had been done.

The young WPc arrived within minutes. He let her in, and was briefing her, when the cleaner, Elaine, arrived with the Italian waiter. He seemed rather sleepy, and suggested he make them all a coffee. Saul thanked him, and said, "How kind of you, I should love one, and I think this officer would as well. I doubt you had time for one at the station, did you?"

"No, sir, I came straight over when Sergeant Graves said. What do you want me to do?"

Saul was impressed with her eagerness and keen attitude. He looked down at her, and smiled. She looked a little less nervous and smiled weakly back.

"There is no need to be scared of me, I don't bite, despite what you have heard! Yes, I can be tough, hard and I do have a bit of a temper, but I only lose it if someone defies me. I doubt you will do that?"

"No, sir, I wouldn't dream of it, but what if I don't know how to do what you ask?"

"Then the fault would be mine, for not explaining properly. I need you to hang on here, until you are relieved. I'd like you to record who comes down for breakfast, and not let any strangers into the pub, unless you clear it with the list I have here. Ah, this seems to be the coffee."

Giuseppe put a tray on the table, and said, "I go get the milk from the fridge, back in a minute."

He moved off into the kitchen, while Elaine handed them the mugs. She looked at Saul, and said, "I went and saw Brenda yesterday evening. She's still very shaken up, said your woman detective went to see her and take a statement from her. Actually, she quite upset her. I do think she could have been a bit more tactful about it. Brenda told me that she believed Major Greywell was actually her natural father, but the woman told her not to be fanciful, and virtually suggested she was attention seeking. Told her to get back to work and stop being a drama queen. I rather resent that, because Brenda has never been like that, she is a very sensible young woman. I've known her since she was small. She's coming in later, and if she feels up to it, she'll help me with the rooms or the laundry."

Before Saul could think of anything to say, there was a resounding crash from the kitchen area, followed by a strangled shriek, and a copious amount of swearing in Italian.

The three of them rushed into the kitchen and on to the fridge at the back of the building. As they rounded the corner, Giuseppe came out, as white as a sheet, and Elaine helped him onto the chair in the neighbouring laundry. There was milk all over the floor, and many broken bottles. Saul looked into the large walk-in fridge, and initially could see nothing amiss, but carefully stepped over the broken milk, and looked round. The young WPc followed him, and said, "Behind you, sir, on the floor, under the bottom shelf."

Saul turned and saw the body of Ruby, scrunched up, and very still. He tentatively felt for a pulse, but the body was cold. He stepped back, and said, "Thank you, are you all right, lass?"

"Yes sir. What do you want me to do?"

"Get back to the phone, call the station, ask for all the usual, and tell them we have another body. When you have done that, come back and see me. I'll stop here, take those two with you."

"Shall I take one of the unbroken bottles of milk with me? I think the waiter and the lady might need a cup of coffee."

"Yes, good girl, what is your name?"

"Tatum Barber, sir, but my friends call me Tate. Are you all right? It was a bit of a shock."

"You will do well in this job, Tate. Yes, I'll be fine. I have seen a few bodies before, you know!"

"Of course you have sir, but I haven't seen many, and never like that. It can still shake anyone up. I'll get on with what you said, sir. I'll take the lady and gentleman with me."

After a brief look around, Saul shut the fridge door and stood outside it. He knew who the woman was, and was cursing himself for her death. If only he'd insisted a watch was kept overnight. His anger began to build. Before long, Tate came back with a cup of coffee in her hand, which she handed to him.

"I thought you might like one, sir. I've done all that, now what do you want me to do?"

"Go and find me a padlock and key, that I can lock this door with. They may have one here, if not, go to the station and ask Sgt Graves to find one. I want all the keys. That is the best way to secure the scene. Bring it to me."

"Certainly. I'll be as quick as I can."

Soon the Scenes of Crime officers had arrived, and the doctor, who confirmed death, and was able to tell Saul that Ruby had been stabbed with a long, thin knife or blade. When several officers had taken control of the site, Saul said to Tate, "Well done, officer! Come back to the station with me, and make a statement; it's all right, I'll help you, I need to make one as well."

As they walked out of the back door, the chef, Paul, came up to them.

"Are you the officer in charge?"

"I am."

"Then I think I need to tell you something, or one of your officers. A couple of things, in fact. I just found out what happened, and last night, I was missing one of my knife set. I looked for it but can't find it anywhere. It is my filleting knife, and it has a white handle, the blade is about nine inches, I think. I temporarily mislaid it yesterday, too. I found it in the sink, in the washing up water. The other thing is, I heard a very interesting conversation between two of the guests the other day, out here in the yard. With what is going on, I think you ought to know. Obviously, I can't get inside the kitchen at the moment to look again for the knife, but I did wonder if it had been thrown in the bin room, or the box room. Do you want me to look for it?"

"No, we will do that. Where were the knives kept?"

"Just inside the kitchen, in the knife blocks. We each have our own set, and mine are worth quite a bit, and I look after them. I missed it just before I left last night, but thought I might have misplaced it; but I've been thinking about it, and I remember putting it away earlier. We don't borrow each other's knives, at all. I thought you should know."

"Thank you. Wait here a moment. Tate, please go in and fetch DS Cannon will you, ask him to deal with this gentleman?"

Paul was taken off to make a statement, and Saul walked back with Tate to the police station. He arrived in the general CID office just before ten, and asked for a general conference at ten thirty. In his office, there were a number of neat files on his desk. Mo knocked on the door, and came in.

"I found all those files you asked for sir, and some others I thought you might be wanting. I heard what happened, what do you want me to do now?"

"Could you make sure young Tate is all right, and get her to have a coffee or something? Then I want you at the conference I am calling. Is DI Allenby in yet?"

"No, not yet, sir. She said last night she was planning to come in about ten. When she does, shall I ask her to come and see you?"

"Mo, please could you wait for her, and bring her directly to my office? Don't tell her what happened last night. I don't want her talking to anyone else. I need to tell her. If I'm elsewhere, wait here with her, please. I have to have something out with her."

"You mean you told her to put someone on duty last night, and she quite deliberately decided not to bother."

Saul looked at Mo, with a dawning respect.

"How do you know that?"

"It's what I would have done. She thinks she knows better than you, she's after your job. She has a lot to learn, especially about manners, sir."

"Explain, please."

"I don't mean no disrespect, I mean, she is a senior officer and all that, but so far she has been insufferably rude to me, Sgt Graves, and the other officers from here. Treats us all like muck off her shoe. I know I don't have half her skills, but she told me yesterday evening that I had no business trying to suck up to you, and I was only in the way. Told me to leave this kind of thing to the experts, not the geriatric club."

"In which she did, no doubt, include me? Out with it, man, I need an honest answer."

"She wasn't very respectful about you, and didn't like it when I told her that she should talk of you with respect."

"Thank you, Mo. I do not think she and I can work together again. I would like to tell you that you have more detective ability in your little finger than she has in her whole body. I need you, Mo, and I am going to ask a favour of you, quite unusual, but I believe in using everyone to their full potential. For all your professed lack of experience in this field, and your years, you have a needle-sharp brain, and an eye for detail. I need someone with me who can see what isn't there. Would you mind reading all the papers relating to this, and telling me what, if anything, does not make sense? I need at least a second view on them."

"I'm sure you see all that, sir,"

"Yes, but you know or see what isn't right, what doesn't fit in, and with your local knowledge, and your experience of life, I would value your input. Yes, I know I have a dozen detectives, some of whom could do it, but I need them out doing other things."

"I'd be pleased to help. Will I have to work with DI Allenby?"

"No. I'll find her something less critical to do, until I can send her back to headquarters."

"I don't want to cause no trouble."

"You are not. I need you. I can do without her, just at the moment."

"She's young, she'll learn. Don't be too hard on her."

Saul retreated to his office, made a few phone calls, and then went down to the CID office. He briefed all the officers on their duties, and asked one of his sergeants to take charge of the office, and allocate actions and nominate a computer operative for the special Murder programme.

"Sir, DI Allenby was doing this. She'll be in soon. Shall I confirm it with her?"

"No. I'll have this done my way from now on. She is an authorised operative isn't she? She can work the computer. Now, get out and interview, and if anyone isn't straight or helpful, bring them in. We know our murderer is still here, and I want them in custody as soon as we can, before we have another death. As soon as I can I will get us more officers to assist, but until the roads are clear we must work with what we have. The problem is, with this case there is too much information, not too little. Everywhere we look, there are suspects. Too many. This person is desperate. As soon as I can, I am going to interview some myself. Due to our predicament, I have included on the team officers you may find strange. Section Officer Mo Tasker will be helping me, and I hope WPc Barber, if she feels up to it.'

"Yes, sir, they'd like to help."

"Good. I know those of you who are experienced will help her. Find out where Brenda Royce is. Ask her to come and see me here. Be gentle with her. I need to talk to her urgently. Dean, Mike, please go and bring in the two Atterthwaite boys; if they won't come willingly, then nick them. Gerry and Todd, please bring in Archie Babble. That should do for starters. Keep me informed."

Saul returned to his office only seconds before Mo came in with Celia. Mo tactfully left, closing the door behind him.

"Sit down, Celia, we need to talk."

"What the hell is going on? I really resent being treated like a junior officer, or even a suspect! How dare you get a bloody special to escort me, as though I was a stranger!"

"Shut up! For your information, Section Officer Tasker has my confidence, which is a sight more than you have. What time did you leave the pub last night?"

Celia glared up at him. "So that is what this is about, because I chose not to waste valuable time, manpower and money on letting some lazy Pc be on duty all night. Just how petty can you get?"

"What time?"

"About half past midnight, a bit later I think."

"According to your desk diary it was 1213 when you signed off. Can you explain how another murder was allowed to take place in the pub last night?"

"What? Who?"

"Before I tell you that, I want a full statement of everything you saw, heard and did there last night. The forms are there, together with all your paperwork and diary. I need to know what you saw and heard, who was where when you left. Only then will we discuss the matter. I was unable to find the statement you took yesterday from Brenda Royce, I take it you have it with you. Hand it over please."

"I took an executive decision, but knew you would treat her with kid gloves. That's why I didn't mention it. I have it in my briefcase, here. You won't get much from her, she has a vivid imagination. Silly woman thought she was related. Talk about trying to get attention! I told her not to waste our time with such nonsense."

"I heard. Did you take this statement before or after I told you to leave her to me?"

"After. I had already decided to visit her, and you must see that we needed the evidence of the discovery of the bodies as soon as we could, to establish a time frame. I'm sorry, guv, but you do pussy-foot around sometimes. It couldn't wait. I don't think you understand that she discovered all three bodies."

"Your arrogance amazes me sometimes, Detective Inspector Allenby. Make that statement, now. Leave nothing out. If you do, I shall have no option but to consider, and treat you, as a suspect. On this occasion, I require you, no, order you to do as you are told. Please do not leave this office until you have done so."

Saul continued to read a file, while she huffed and puffed, and then reluctantly began to write a statement. He caught several withering stares from her. She was emanating fury. He returned her stare, with a calm and cold one, and pretended not to see her attempts to make him uneasy. She was behaving like a truculent child, but as her predicament was awkward, he quite understood.

After half an hour, she said, "I need to visit the toilet. I'll be back in a minute."

"Then you had better finish it quickly. I will not allow you to talk to anyone else until you have completed it. You are skating on very thin ice, Celia, don't take me for a fool. At this moment, believe it or not, I am attempting to save your career, not damage it. Now get on!"

Fifteen minutes later, she handed him a written statement which he read, and he nodded. "If that is the truth, then sign it. Is it?"

"It is all I can remember. I don't think I have left anything important out."

"I didn't ask you for what you considered important, I asked you for everything. What else is there?"

"Well, that odious woman, Mrs Greywell, seemed very drunk; not surprising, considering the amount of gin she had in front of her. I think she was bought drinks by everyone at some stage. The barman will know. I've put in who was talking to who."

"Then put that in, please, it may be very important, I think it is."

It took another ten minutes before she once again handed the statement to Saul. He held out his hand, and said, "And Brenda Royce's statement, and any others you may have in your briefcase, please?"

She rather truculently opened her briefcase, and handed him a wad of statements. He watched, and said, "What else do you have in there?"

She blushed, and then stood up, and tipped the contents onto his desk. He picked up a wad of the papers he had copied and given to her the previous day.

"I know you said they had to stay here, but I was trying to save time by reading them before I came in this morning. I have to make some decisions of my own, you know! They were quite safe, I assure you. I never let them out of my sight. I suppose you'll make a big thing of it. Why don't you just stick me on a disciplinary, make me look small in front of the others! It's what you have always wanted, you have always resented me."

"You wished to visit the bathroom. Compose yourself and come back, and I will explain why I am so angry. I have every right to be. If I wished to make a fool of you, do you think I would have made sure this was in private, not in front of the squad?"

Celia slammed out of the office, and returned after ten minutes. She had obviously been crying. He indicated the seat, and as she sat down, he closed the door, and said, "It may interest you to know that Ruby Greywell was killed last night in the pub, and her body was placed in the fridge of the kitchen. Had an officer been on duty last night, that would not have happened. I am not saying she wouldn't have been killed, but a police presence would have stopped it being done that way. While you were there, did you see anyone unusual go into the kitchen?"

"During the evening, no, but I did see that man Windle coming out of there, earlier that evening. I actually asked him why he had been in there. He said he had gone to fetch a cloth, he even had a tea towel in his hand. Blue and white, small check. He wiped up a spillage on one of the tables, where Ruby Greywell was. He had been talking to her."

"Did he return the towel?"

"I didn't see him do so, but it wasn't there later. Sir, I'm sorry, I thought I was doing the right thing."

"I'm sure you did. Celia, you must learn to listen to others. I know you think me a doddering old fool, but you must accept that there are things you do not know yet. I'm far from perfect, I know that, I make mistakes, I did yesterday. I thought I could trust you to carry out my suggestions. Now we know how we really feel about each other, I think we should not work together again. For the remainder of the enquiry, I want you to take over collating all the information on the computer, and help run the office. I know you will consider this a demotion, but you do understand that I can no longer trust you to do as I ask?"

"You can trust me!"

"Probably, but it isn't just that. For your information, Brenda Royce is the natural daughter of Cecil Greywell, and stands to inherit a great deal of money, but whether she knew that, I'm not sure. You have seriously upset her, and now, I'll find it twice as hard to get her to be straight with me, and that is down to you. You must not ride roughshod over people and their feelings, just because you think it will hurry things up."

"Is this going to damage my promotion chances?"

"What do you think? It will certainly delay them. How can I give you an honest appraisal, and not mention it? In many ways, you are an excellent officer, but I have yet to see you consider anyone but yourself. It isn't all about your results. You think no one can do anything better than you, or do it another way. Your main failing is to be blind to the talents other people have, that you don't. Section Officer Tasker, for example. He is a wise, observant and dedicated man, with a great deal of local knowledge. He knows a lot about life, and I need to use him. For all he is a lowly Special Constable, that you apparently despise, he is an asset. If you want respect from others, first give it to them."

Celia looked at him, and said, "Is that how you do it? There is not one member of the squad that doesn't adore you. They don't like me, I know that, I thought they resented me because I was a woman, or because you did."

"No, I didn't resent you. I did try, Celia, to show you, without making myself a dictatorial boss, how to get the best out of the team. Now you have dropped all of us in the shit, because you thought you knew better than any of us. Most of the squad have been doing this job for years. They know me, and how I work, as I know them. You were posted to me for a reason, to learn. You have many abilities. It was hoped you would take on board other methods. Do you want to carry on in CID?"

"Yes, I do. It is all I ever wanted. Now what do I do?"

"After this case, I want you to take a bit of leave, think things through. You have the ability to replace me, eventually, but not yet. For the time being, run the office, and consider those around you. Watch, listen, learn. DC Oakes, for example. He comes over as brusque, almost aggressive. Have you ever seen him talking to suspects? How do you think he gets so much information? He is a big bear. Soft inside, tough on the outside. It works. Then there is WDC Pellow. She seems pathetic, almost weedy. That woman has a will of steel, but she gets her results, because she makes people feel sorry for her, they think she can do no harm to anything. Then DS Mullins; he is quite a joker, nothing ever seems to get to him. He gives the appearance of never listening or hearing anything you ever say. Makes a joke of everything. I admit, I found it rather annoying at first, still do, occasionally, but he hears everything. He doesn't miss a trick. He has a phenomenal memory, photographic, certainly, but it is more than that. He doesn't always know where to draw the line with his jokes, but he is invaluable."

"I had no idea. You know all about all of us, don't you? How do I get to know these things?"

"By observing. Each of the team has their own strengths and weaknesses. I use them for what they are best at. You, for example, have a special ability with logistics. You organize well. You have an ordered mind. You have little or no imagination, and cannot accept that others have. Intuition is something quite alien to you. When you have been with any of the team, you have always had to be the one in control. I suggest that you sit back and watch them. Go out with them, see how they do what they do. They have been working for you, because they have had to, not because they want to. You have built walls around you so high, that no one can see the real person inside. I know why you are like that, and I understand, but they don't."

"What do you know about me? I've never allowed my private life to be discussed."

"Quite a lot. You are basically insecure, lonely, and resentful of others' popularity. At some time you have been badly hurt by a relationship, and hate rejection. You have an elder brother, who has done very well in his profession; he is an academic, a professor at Oxford, and your parents think the world of him, and have never acknowledged your achievements, which are considerable. You feel the need constantly to prove yourself. Am I right?"

"Yes, but how did you find all that out? Especially about my brother? That isn't even on my personal record!"

"I happen to know him. He told me a lot. I have even met your parents. He was tutor to my eldest son, at Oxford. I didn't pry, I promise. He is very proud of you. Your father has never seen anyone but him."

"Who else have you told about this?"

"No one. I don't tell anyone what they don't need to know. Now, we have some murders to solve. Will you help me, by taking over the office? While you do it, watch and learn about the others."

"Are you not going to put me an a disciplinary? I would someone who had done it to me."

"You made a bad judgement. I don't see how it would help. I think we have ironed out a few problems. If you can take them on board, things might be a bit easier for all of us. Agreed?"

"The others must know I made a cock up. How do I face them?"

"Admit you are human, say I have sorted it out, and if they have a problem with it, refer them to me. They all know better than to push me. So should you, now. I have some interviewing to do. Before you start on the office I want you to do something for me. If you would, please take Section Officer Tasker, treat him with great respect, and then time some walks for me. I have listed them here, he knows where they are. You could do a lot worse than to unburden yourself on him, while you do it. He is the soul of discretion, and a very wise man."

"In other words, you are giving me time to control myself and a solid shoulder to cry on? Thank you, for being so understanding. Do you know, the only thing I really know about you is that you have never failed to solve a murder case you have been on. I don't know anything about the personal lives of those I work with. I need to, obviously. You are telling me it is necessary."

"It is what makes us tick. When I am a little less busy, you can talk to me. I will listen. I'll help if I can. We all have problems, me included. Go on, find Mo."

Chapter Eleven

Saul went down to the cell block and saw the duty custody officer, and then went to an interview room. He sat down in front of Archie Babble.

After the procedure had been explained by DS Mullins, and the introductions made, Saul let DS Mullins start the interview. After ten minutes or so, during which time they established where Babble had been, Saul waited for a pause, and said, "Archie, you threatened and even assaulted Greywell. He is now dead, murdered. On the night he was murdered, you were seen, not far from The Golden Lion, about the time the murder occurred. I would like an explanation."

"Yup, you're quite right. I did threaten him, and assault him, I put my hands up to that. I am glad he is dead, but I didn't do it. If you find out who did, I'd like to shake their hand. When I had a go at him, I was drunk. I haven't been in there since, Tim the barman banned me for a month. Look, I'll be straight with you. I did think about it, but thought better of it. He ruined me once, if I had killed him, he would have done it again. I'm not clever, I know that, I could never have got away with it. When the snow was forecast, I got called in to help grit the roads. I went in about eight that night. By half one, it was pointless carrying on, because it was settling so fast. The foreman called us back, and told us to come in the next morning. I put the gritter in the yard behind Victoria Hall, and walked up to the square. I walked so far, even saw Sgt Graves on patrol. I didn't actually want to meet him, he gave me a hard time about having a go. I remembered I had left my baccy in the cab, so I went back for it. There weren't many folk around. I saw young Brenda, and Sgt Graves again, but I don't think he saw me, and then when I was going past the Brass Cat, I did stop and think about going in, but someone came out from the back yard, so I hurried on home. I reckon that was about two."

"Who was it you saw coming out of the pub?"

"Don't know his name, I think it was one of Greywell's lot. Big chap, but I didn't get that close."

"Would you recognize him?"

"No, don't think so, big man, tall, but that is all I can tell you. He had a big coat and a hood up."

"Did you see anyone else that night?"

"I heard someone following me for a while. I turned off down Station Road, and who ever it was went on towards Duke Street. I saw a figure, male I think, not the same chap what came out the pub, slimmer. Not as tall."

"Did you see where the man coming from the pub went?"

"Yes, but it was odd. He came out, looked up and down the road, walked up to the corner, by the nick, and then came back to the pub yard. He didn't go in, he turned right down into the yard, you know where they put the boxes and rubbish. I moved off then, didn't seem him no more."

"Was it Cecil Greywell?"

"No, I'd have known him, I'd have had a go at him, but it were taller than him."

"Who can confirm where you were that night? Was there anyone at home?"

"The foreman, and the rest of the crew, but I live alone, with me dog."

"Would you mind giving us your fingerprints?"

"You've already got them, but no, if you want them, I've no reason to say no."

"Where were you last night?"

"Out with the gritter, all night, from nine last night to about four this morning. I'd not say no to getting a bit of kip, if I can go?"

"Give my officer your prints, and then take yourself off to bed."

Saul had barely time to finish his notes and do the paperwork for the interview, before Jack Atterthwaite was shown in. A new tape was started, and after a few explanatory comments, Saul asked, "I know why you hated Cecil Greywell. Did you kill him?"

"No. I would have liked to, very much, but he has caused my family enough anguish already. I'm not surprised someone did. Before you ask, Jo and I were in town that night. We both got as pissed as rats, at the Talbot. We left there a bit late, and decided the safest thing was to walk home. We would have got a taxi, but there were none. In the end, we rang my wife, and she picked us up just past the golf course, at the top of Buker Brow, with the Land Rover."

"Did you visit the Lion at all?"

"Earlier in the evening, yes, we had a pint in the pool room, but Greywell and his mob came down, so we left. I wanted nothing more to do with him. Adrian Graves had warned me off a few days before, told me to keep out of the way. Good man, Adrian."

"Would you mind if we took your fingerprints?"

"No, if it helps. I'll tell you now, you will find them on Greywell's case, and possibly in his room, five I think it was."

"How come?"

"Before I knew who he was, he asked me to take his case up there for him. I did, to help Tim out. I put it on the case stand in the room, and then switched the light on, and moved the waste bin that I had stumbled into in the dark. I've nothing to hide, Mr Catchpole, but I don't want you to catch the killer, if I am honest. They have done humanity a favour."

"Is there anything else you have seen or heard, anything strike you as unusual?"

"Yes, if you must know, there is. That first day, when I took Greywell's case up, I was watching the party in the bar. It was before I knew who they were. There was a big, heavy man, and I thought I'd seen him before. It's been nagging me. Anyway, I saw him again, that night. He was outside the Lion, I saw him go into the yard. He just seemed creepy. Then, I was in town last night, and I saw him again, walking round the square. It was quite late. I was coming away from the NFU meeting. I'd stopped on at the Rugby club for a chat with old Morrison, who farms up from me. I think I saw this chap put something in the waste bin on the corner of the Shambles. Looked like a little bottle. I drove past as he did so."

"Do you know who this chap is?"

"I think someone called him Oliver, and I think the name is something like Winkle. I've not met him to speak to."

"Could you try to remember where you have seen him before? It may be important."

"I asked Jo, he don't remember him at all. I think I remember him from a long time ago. He may have visited my dad at our other farm. If I am right, my mother was terrified of him, not sure why, but I don't remember him by that name. I thought it was Winchester then. I may be wrong, it was a long time ago."

"Would your father remember?"

"I doubt it. I'd rather you left him out of it. I'll ask him for you, and I'll give you a ring."

"Thank you. Please, give your fingerprints to my colleague, and then you are free to go. Thank you for coming in to see me, which I understand you did of your own free will."

"I sort of got the impression that if I didn't, we'd come in anyway. So Jo and I came in, to get it sorted."

While Saul was waiting for the next visitor, he spoke to the pathologist again. He made notes, and then collected several faxes from the machine in the general office and sat looking at them. As he was reading, Mo and Celia came in, chatting like old friends. Mo winked at him, and Celia smiled, "Hello, you two, look I have news for you. Read this, it rather complicates matters, I think. Go get a coffee, and join me in the squad room. It seems we have at least three killers. Oh bother, that does put the cat amongst the pigeons!"

Saul went to his office, collected some papers, and then made his way to the squad room. In the corridor, he was met by Celia.

"Are you all right?"

"Yes, sir, I am, I just want to say thank you. I'm so sorry I let you down. He's a lovely man, isn't he? More like the father I didn't have."

"Good. Now, I have some very interesting facts from forensic, and I've also heard from York. Could you check this list of vehicle numbers for me? Then I want to know where the nearest magistrate is, to obtain some search warrants, and after that, while we are confirming alibis, we need to get going on the Greywell lot. Please, Celia, could you arrange for a constant watch to be kept on this man Windle? Now the roads are clearing, he may just try to get away, and I want him to go, but if he does, I want him watched. I have just sent out several lads to search a couple of locations. I am hoping we may find something. The first is the yard of the pub, again, not the most pleasant task, as it includes the rubbish, but the other is the waste bin in the Market Place, all of them but first the one by the Shambles, that I believe is the building in the middle. Can I leave that with you?"

"Yes, you can, I won't let you down again. I take it you have eliminated Babble and the two farming lads?"

"Not exactly, but I don't think they are the killers. Has Ruby Greywell's body gone yet?"

"Yes, went ages ago, they were going to do the PM straight away."

"I think we will have to wait for the toxicology report. When I looked at her eyes, I thought they looked drugged. Who is interviewing Tim and Giuseppe?"

"It's been done. Tim White was very specific, very accurate. He is observant, and was paying great attention, which is more than I was. He was able to tell us exactly who bought what drinks, and kept a note. He even timed them! Look, Brenda

Royce is coming in, I think I should apologise to her. Would that be all right?"

"Yes, it might be very helpful if you do. Do you want to sit in on the interview?"

"Would you mind? Mo said that he could learn a lot from you, which meant that I could too."

"Well done, you are listening!"

The squad room was filling up when they went in. Some more officers had managed to get in, as the roads had been cleared. There was a respectful silence as Saul sat on the desk, and said, "Right, troops, pin back your lug holes and listen! We have a lot of work to do in very little time. DI Allenby will give out your tasks at the end of this meeting. Then I want all of them done as fast as possible. Jack, what is the weather forecast?"

"More bloody snow, and already the main A65 is closed, in both directions, a few miles down the road. One side with a major accident, the other already blocked with snow. The back roads are pretty impassable, have been for days."

"Yes, that is what worries me. If our murderer is trapped here, we may just have another fatality. Tate, will you do something for me?"

"Me, sir? Yes, if I can."

"In a little while, I intend to talk to all the Greywell party at the pub, or here. I am going to tell them exactly what the situation is about Major Greywell's will. Brenda Royce is the main beneficiary of it. They do not know that yet. When they do, and I think it will be a grave shock to most of them, I think that she might be in great danger. If I am right, and this is about money, then someone might want her out of the way. It is possible, of course that she is the murderer, but I don't think so. I want you to stick to her like glue, unless relieved, and then it

138

will be by me or DI Allenby here. It will mean staying over at her place, or going with her wherever she goes. Can you get all you need, and that will include a radio, and a mobile phone? I want an hourly ring in or report that all is well. Go home, get what you need, and then come back to see me."

"Yes, sir, you want me to go now?"

"Please. Now, Mo, I need you to do some reading for me. Caleb, have all the rooms been searched again?"

"Yes, but we found very little. The older cleaner, Elaine, she did mention something unusual, it may not be connected, but I think you should know."

"Go on."

"The cleaners keep all their tips in the cleaners' cupboard on the first floor landing. Because of previous problems when they had a thief on the staff, they actually record the numbers of the notes they have in there. She asked if we had removed it when we searched. We hadn't. It was there last time we searched, but it has now gone. She gave me the numbers of the notes that had gone, there was about £120 in there. When we searched room eleven, we found several of those notes in the purse of one of the daughters of the murdered woman. We haven't said anything, but it seems that she must have taken it. One of the notes, a tenner, had a consecutive number to the money we found in Major Greywell's room. The cleaner said he gave it to Brenda as a tip. It seems that he also gave the daughter some money from his wallet, as there are other notes in the same series in her purse. I asked the cleaner if she wanted to make a theft report, and she said yes. What do I do?"

"Arrest the girl concerned. Is it the one with previous for theft?"

"Yes, sir, it is."

"Then go and do that now. That takes at least one out of the equation, and temporarily out of danger. Take one of the ladies with you and bring her back here."

As each officer went off to do their allotted tasks, Saul and Celia went to an office and sat down with Brenda. Celia gave a very gracious apology, and then Saul said, "Thanks for coming in. This has been a dreadful time for you, I know, and I think you are dealing with it very bravely. You told my officer that you believed you were the natural daughter of Cecil Greywell. Why?"

Brenda told him, at length, everything that had happened over the previous days. She then told him about her mother, and how she had reacted. Saul listened, and they carried on and asked Brenda about the evening when she had gone walking in the snow. She told them what she had seen and done, and how Sgt Graves had walked her so far, and then she had gone home. Saul interrupted her.

"Who did you see, apart from Mr Graves, that night?"

Brenda paused, and then said, "I'm not sure I saw anyone. I thought I saw someone I knew, but it can't have been him. I did see another man, but I have no idea who it was."

"This person you thought you knew, who was it?"

"I'm not sure and I'd rather not say. I think it was just the storm, I was seeing things."

She looked up at Saul and met the penetrating stare of two blue eyes. She blushed. She looked over at Celia, to see her looking at Saul as well. There was a long silence.

"We'll leave that for now. Did you go into the pub?"

"No, I didn't. Yes, I have a back door key, but it was in my other coat pocket."

"Did you know that the day before, Major Greywell visited a local solicitor and remade his will?"

"No, I had no idea, but in any case it wouldn't be any of my business. I admit, I was a little curious about him, but I didn't want to get to know him, mainly for my mother's sake."

"Then the fact that he has left the bulk of his considerable fortune to you, is news?"

"What, that can't be right! He didn't even know me, or about me, except those last few days. You're not serious?"

"Very serious. If you did know, or were told, you must tell me, Brenda. Have you any idea of how rich he was?"

"No, and I don't care, or want his bloody money. He was never there when I was small, I don't want anything to do with him, or his filthy money."

There was no doubt that her surprise and shock were genuine. She was very upset, and sat thinking for a while.

"Do I have to take it?"

"Yes, but I am sure you can give it all away if you want to. There is no doubting the validity of the will. It will take some time, but we are looking at millions, I believe. You could do a lot of good with that, you know."

"I suppose I could, yes, but it doesn't seem fair. Who else knew about this?"

"I don't know. It does, however, put me in a quandary. I don't want to frighten you, but if he was murdered for his money, you could be in considerable danger, young lady. Whoever is behind his murder will not hesitate to strike again, they did last night. For that reason, I have arranged for you to be protected. A young woman officer is going to be with you, all the time, until I consider you are safe."

"Thank you, this is very frightening. I should be all right, I don't think any of them know where I live."

"I wouldn't assume anything. This is a small town, and I won't take chances with you. Will you accept my protection?"

"If I must, but I could go to stay with my mother and step-father."

"Would you rather?"

Brenda thought about it, and then remembered that she had seen her stepfather that night. She further remembered the conversation she had had with him about Cecil. He had known, she was sure of it. She wondered what had he been doing that night, out in the snow.

"No, I need to be at home, I have two cats. I want to be in my own place. This whole thing will have upset my mother lots, and I don't want to add to her worries. The policewoman will have to kip on the settee, I don't have a big place. Who is it?"

"Young Tatum, do you know her?"

"Yes, I do, she's fun. She has just joined the hockey team. I don't mind her, at all. How long will this last?"

"Not too long, I'm sure. You see, I think we are very close to finding out who one of our killers is. You must be honest with me, because if I am to protect you, I need to know everything. Tatum will take you home, and I want you to tell her if anything is the slightest bit unusual. Is that a deal?"

"Yes, all right."

They got up to go, and Celia went to find Tatum. Saul looked down at the frightened girl, and said softly, "It would help if you told me who it was you saw that night. It is obviously someone you are protecting, but you're not sure, are you? Not sure you can trust them? As soon as you can, tell me, and I can eliminate them, but whoever it is, please, don't trust them. Here is my number, tell me if you want to talk. It isn't a good idea to hide things from us, even out of loyalty. I'll work it out, but you could save me time. Think on it, lass, because it may be quite innocent."

He knew he was right, he could almost see her thinking it through. She blushed again, and then went off with Tatum. Saul went to find Mo.

"Mo, does young Brenda Royce have a boyfriend?"

"No, not that I know of. She did have, several, but they have all moved on."

"Then what man might she be fond enough of to protect?"

"Man, well the only one I know of is her stepdad, Tim Royce, or her younger brothers of course."

"I see. How are you getting on with those statements and papers?"

"Not too bad, but there are one or two things that are not right about a couple, that I know of. These faxed copies of the papers from York, that were found in Greywell's house, in the safe; there is at least one obvious one missing, Doreen Royce, Williams as she used to be. He has documented all the dealings he had where it seems that he bested anyone. Not just here, but all over the place. The two years he lived at Austwick are covered quite comprehensively, but there are pages missing, and if I remember things correctly, they would have been when he was accused of rape. Now, I turned up the original file, and I'm right."

"What else springs to mind?"

"He tells about the business with the Atterthwaite family, and then he deals with the other farmers, but he mentions Archie

143

Babble. In all of them, he does, to a certain extent, justify what he did. It seems that Archie never paid him a penny. He says that it was the only occasion that he had been outwitted, and lost money. Then there are the missing pages, and he stated he moves over to the York area, but I noticed that he refers to the sum of money he paid to Doreen Williams, as compensation for what he did to her. He also mentions that she wrote him a letter saying she wished nothing more to do with him. There are several references to an allowance paid to Tobias, but I can find nothing else to back it up. Tobias is in inverted commas, so I assume it is a fictitious name for someone. This Tobias seems to have made considerable demands. But nowhere can I find any papers involving him. I wonder who he is. I would also have thought there would be something on Windle, and more on Greville, but there are whole pages missing. Then, much later, he mentions someone asking for money to set up a medical business, and threatening to disclose something.

"In it he says that he has already explained in his account about his feelings of guilt at what he did. He says, in a later paragraph, that he only ever took advantage of the greed of others. I'm sure you noticed that, but when he starts to explain, the pages are missing."

"Yes, interesting, isn't it? Very conveniently, all means of identifying this person have been removed. Have you read all of that yet?"

"Not yet. This statement that young Brenda made, the first one, that Celia took, she made no mention about her possible connection to Greywell. Why not?"

"I think that might have been down to the statement taker. Can you note down anything that occurs to you?"

"I am. Do we know what the murder weapon was with Greywell?"

"Not yet. I had forensics on earlier. They are pretty convinced that the man from room twelve, Cordwell, had a fight with the man under the stairs, Grimsdale. It looks very much as if Grimsdale killed Cordwell, but now we have to work out who killed Grimsdale, why, and if it is the same person that killed the other two. Keep reading, please, Mo, your input is invaluable."

Chapter Twelve

After a hurried lunch, a sandwich and a coffee, during which time Saul read the notes that his son had given him, he went down to the interview rooms again. Greville Greywell was sitting smoking a cheroot, waiting impatiently. Saul walked in, and sat down with one of the Detective Sergeants.

Saul cautioned Greywell, and said, "Have you been offered a solicitor?"

"Yes, but I don't need one. You have a cheek, keeping us hanging round like this. I have decided to go home as soon as I can. Not only have I lost my brother, but now my wife has been killed. I don't think it is safe for me to stay here. I might be next. Then your officers arrest one of my daughters on some trumped up charge. I demand to see her. She needs a solicitor, not me."

"She is adult, and has been advised of her rights. I agree, I doubt it is wise for you to stay in the pub. What happened last night? Please, tell me your movements, and those of anyone else that you can remember. Don't waste my time glossing over things you would rather not divulge. I know you had at least one argument with your wife. What was it about?"

"If you must know, she almost accused me of cheating her and Cecil. She was worried about some jewellery she wears sometimes. She had it on yesterday. Cecil brought it back from

Italy, years ago, and loaned it to me, for display. For some reason, he thought there was something rather unusual about it. She should never have worn it, and I had told her so. The waiter, the Italian chap, he obviously recognised where it was from. He seemed very distressed over it. She was being very mysterious about something. Told me that she had seen something the night before, something important. Then she said she ought to tell you lot, but wondered if it was the right thing to do. When I asked her what she meant, she said she knew who had killed Cecil, at least she thought she did. She said she had seen someone with Cecil, late. Seen them knocking on his door. Wanted this person to talk to her. She asked me how much it should be worth to say nothing. I told her it would be both foolish and dangerous to play that game. I warned her that she could end up dead too. Obviously she didn't listen to me. During yesterday evening, she talked to everyone, at some stage."

"You have already told us your side of the events leading up to Cecil's death. Do you wish to add anything, or change that story in any way?"

"If you must know, I suspected Ruby might have had a hand in it. He threatened both our daughters, and she is fiercely defensive about them. I was wrong."

"Any reason for that?"

"Yes, and no. We have been having a lot of differences recently. Love died for us long ago. We stayed together more from habit, and convenience. I didn't wish her any harm, don't get me wrong, but I did suspect she had someone else, but I don't know who it was."

"Did you visit your brother the night he died?"

"Me, no, I didn't go near him. Never even went into his room. I had no need to."

"Then how do you explain your fingerprints on the marble topped table in room five?"

There was a long silence. Saul watched Greville, who eventually looked up, and said, "Oh, yes, I remember, I did go in. When I first got here, to ask Cecil to explain why we were summoned here. I stood by that table, and put my hand on it when I bent to pick up a packet of cigarettes I had dropped."

"Why did you really take your car out that night?"

"I told you."

"No, you neglected to mention the person you were meeting in that lay-by at Hellifield. We traced Gerry, and he said you were with another man when he picked you up. He has given us an excellent description of this man, and I know who it is. I suggest you tell me."

"I met a stranger, he stopped to see if I was all right, and then the lorry came along."

"Mr Greywell, don't take me for a fool. You knew this man, and he knew you. I have even traced his car. He is being interviewed at this moment."

"No, he was a friendly chap, but we didn't know each other."

"Then I see little point in continuing this interview until we can find out what he has to say. When your car was searched, we found some very interesting things. We have since checked up on them. Until you can be straight with us, and start telling me the truth, I have to consider why you are lying to us. You know what we have found in your car?"

"No."

"Under the front passenger seat were a quantity of drugs, which we suspect is crack cocaine. I am arresting you on suspicion of possession, with intent to supply, Class A prohibited drugs."

Saul cautioned him, and said, "Search him and lock him up, as far from his daughter as is possible."

Saul got up and left the room, and after a visit to the Gents, he returned to find the detective.

"Did he say anything more?"

"Yes, said his wife had a habit, and the drugs were for her. He was very shaken, I think. What did you make of what he said?"

"He is lying, especially about being in the room. I asked both Brenda and Elaine if they had polished that table every day, and they both told me they had, and always did. What he said about his wife was very interesting. There was sufficient truth in it, but I think he knows it was overheard. She was obviously trying to blackmail the killer. It could just as easily have been him, and by telling us that, he was hoping to divert our attention from him. He is not out of the frame yet."

"Sir, who did he meet?"

"I wish I knew. Someone in a Land Rover. The truck driver doesn't know. He is looking at some photos now. Let him stew for a while. What did the daughter say about the theft?"

"Admitted it, she took the money from the cleaners' cupboard. She also says her uncle gave her some money the night he was killed. She was quite talkative, I understand. Put Windle in the room with Cecil, quite late. What are you thinking about all this, sir?"

"That is difficult to explain. I believe that Grimsdale killed Cordwell, but Grimsdale was a small man, and Cordwell was a very fit, ex army commando. From the state of Grimsdale, there was obviously a hell of a fight. Someone was helping Grimsdale, and then I think they had to silence him. Then they killed Cecil. According to the pathologist, his throat was cut with great strength, and he had bruises that made it look as if two persons were involved again. If Ruby saw something, it seems she wasn't sure of herself, what evidence she had, and was fishing to see who she could catch out. She was knifed, very expertly, in the back of the neck. She put up no resistance at all, the pathologist thinks she was drugged. Fortunately, all the glasses she drank from were still in the bar, and have gone off for examination."

"So you think there are two or more killers?"

"Yes, I do, but there are so many suspects, the whole investigation is strewn with massive red herrings. The more we find out, the wider the field becomes. Those with motives for killing Cecil are legion. My list of suspects grows by the hour."

"Who is on it?"

"Archie Babble, The Atterthwaite lads, Adrian Graves, Brenda Royce, even Wendy whatever her name is. Now the Italian waiter is on it, about the jewellery, not to mention those of the family party who are still alive. Someone is very stealthily moving round us, in a fog of suspects. If there are two or more, they will have provided alibis for each other. Then, as rank outsiders, there are the families of the other people who Cecil Greywell destroyed years ago, not to mention the woman he allegedly raped, or her husband. I wonder?"

"So what do we do now?"

"Await the results of the search warrants. I think most of the statements have been taken. I need you to help me interview. I think we will take the young vet, Ted Arbuthnot, next."

"Why?"

"Because I think he knows something, he's not sure what, but something is worrying him. He and his sister strike me as the best of the bunch."

Pc Ord came down the corridor with a message, which he handed to Saul. Having read it, Saul said, "He has saved me the trouble, he wants to talk to me. Thinks he needs to tell me something."

Over a coffee, Saul listened to everything that Ted told him. When he had finished, Saul asked, "What was it that your uncle told you, when you were talking to him up on Castleberg?"

"He confirmed to me something that I have always suspected, but never liked to consider, about my mother. I do not wish to be disloyal to her, but you need to know what he said. I'm not saying I believe him, but it is a possibility. If I tell you, I need your assurance that she will never be prosecuted for it."

Ted told them, and then made a full statement, signed it, and then said, "I feel especially nervous about putting up at the Lion any longer. With your permission, I have booked in at the Vine Guest House, and so has my sister, Alana."

"Yes, that is fine with us. I would ask you not to leave Settle without informing me, but as we are once again snowed in, I think you might have problems doing a bunk. Who else have you told about moving there?"

"Only Alana. I haven't even told my mother, and I don't intend to. She has been as thick as thieves with both Oliver and Greville, and there is something going on there, I'm not sure I want to know what it is. Fond as I am of my mother, who was, incidentally, not a sister to Uncle Cecil, she was adopted, but I do know she was something like a cousin. I will tell you that she is not the weak little woman she portrays. She is as hard as nails. I found out, while I was here, that she has been accepting money from me, Alana, as well as her widow's pension, as well as a more than generous allowance Cecil gave her that she always denied ever receiving. Cecil told me, how true this is I don't know, that mother dearest was very comfortably off, and had a decent private pension, not to mention owning several properties that she rents out, that she has been using Oliver to administer. Cecil even suggested that she and Oliver had something going between them, but I doubt it. Oliver smells, and my mother is most fastidious. He also told me that Oliver was worth looking at, that he had a lot of fingers in a lot of pies, and had been blackmailing, him, Cecil, for years."

"What else did he say about the party?"

"I know what hold he had over Miles, I'm afraid I told Alana what it was. Miles has a drug addiction, or had, but he has kicked it; but he was afraid to tell Alana so, thought she would kick him over. I doubt she will. Cecil also told me that Colin, his junior accountant, and his father, are both on the sex offenders register, having downloaded a large amount of Child Porn from the Internet. That is the hold he had over them! Bill, the chauffeur, he was in the army under Uncle Cecil, and something happened when they were in Italy that binds them together. He wouldn't say what, but he said they none of them visit churches or religious establishments, because of it. I think, but I have no evidence, that they stole something together, and I think Greville knows what it was. Uncle Cecil told me that he once found Oliver going through some very personal papers. He told me that Oliver knows a lot, about a lot of people, and said I should never trust him, that he wasn't quite what he made himself out to be."

"What was the relationship between Cecil and Charlie?"

"I don't know, but I do suspect that there was something that held them together. I know that Charlie had been in the army, but not with my uncle. Charlie, although small, was very fit, and very strong. I always considered him a slime ball, he had this annoying habit of moving silently, and you never knew if he was listening. He told Uncle Cecil almost everything that went on. He's been around for as long as I can remember. When we were kids, we used to call him the smiling assassin, which for some reason, Uncle Cecil found very amusing. He once told me we were not far off the mark. Quite what he meant, I don't know."

"Did your uncle tell you anything about his son, Percy, or your brother, Wilfred?"

"Wilfred, yes, but all he said about Percy was that he was weak, and not all there. I rather like Percy, actually. He has hidden strengths. I happen to know he told his father to go to hell the other day. Uncle Cecil was pleasantly surprised. Some time ago, Uncle Cecil settled a lot on Percy, to offset inheritance tax, but I don't know the details."

"And Wilfred?"

"Before I tell you that, I need that assurance about protecting my mother."

"I can promise nothing. Let me tell you what I, and others, think. I think that Wilfred is not just your cousin, he is also your half-brother. I suspect that your mother was either raped or coerced in some way by your uncle, and Wilfred is the result."

"I think you had better ask her. I only know what I was told, which is about what you just said. I have a question for you, now. Do you know the details of my uncle's will?"

"I do. He made several wills recently, and the last, and only correct one was made the day before he died. Why is it so important for you to know what was in it?"

"I know for a fact I'll get nothing, and I am quite happy with that. Alana wants nothing either, but my mother is worried she'll be chucked out of the house. I do think the family has a right to know."

"I agree with you. I intend to talk to you all after I have finished interviews."

"What is the big secret?"

"I fear for the safety of the main beneficiary."

"I see. You are convinced that this killer may strike again?"

"Yes, I am. I believe all this is about money."

"In which case, I don't want to know the details of the will. I am not the killer, and I want whoever it is caught. Does anyone else know the details?"

"The solicitor, and myself, at the moment."

"Then tell whoever it is you suspect, and see what they do."

"I had considered that, but can you keep this to yourself?"

"I will. I won't even tell my sister, who is really the only one I care for now I know what really happened."

While Ted made a written statement, Saul went to another room where he read several notes left on his desk. He smiled to himself, and wrote a couple of memos and wrote up his desk diary. Julia was shown in. Once the preliminaries were over, Saul said, "Mrs Arbuthnot, please don't waste my time by hiding anything, no matter how ancient or unimportant or even embarrassing it may be to you. Who is the father of your son, Wilfred?"

"My late husband, Walter Arbuthnot, of course. In any case it is nothing to do with you."

"I was told you were an intelligent woman, but you are not behaving as such. Was Cecil Greywell the father? It should be quite easy to prove with a DNA test."

"You wouldn't! I would never agree to it, nor would Wilfred."

"He has already agreed to do so. Incest is a serious offence, and as a suspect for such an offence, we can take a DNA sample from you. Stop wasting my time. You are behaving as if you were a willing partner to it, if so, then you are in serious trouble. Tell us what happened, and then we know where we stand."

"Damn you! All right. I was very drunk, Walter was overseas, and there had been a party. Cecil was also drunk, I think. He came up to my room to see if I was all right, at least that was what he said, and then he started mucking about, and the next thing I knew, I woke up beside him. I never agreed. Walter had been home on leave not long before, and we decided to keep it a secret. I felt disgusted, and ashamed. If I had cried rape, Cecil would have chucked me and the kids out. All right, I will tell you, Walter suspected, and he wanted me to have an abortion, but I refused. He went off, and was killed in action. I never knew if he meant to be, or not. I do know he told Greville of his suspicions. Greville told me last week that he knew. Oliver did too. He blackmailed me into letting him run my few meagre properties. I've been paying him through the nose for years."

"When you met your brother Greville in the woods by the river last week, what was in the package you exchanged with him?"

"How the hell did you know about that? If you must know he asked for some special jewellery that Cecil kept at home, which Ruby wanted. He said he would say nothing if I gave it to him."

"Did you talk with Ruby last night?"

"Yes, I did. She was wearing the stuff, which was very dangerous, and Greville knew it. I asked her not to wear it in

155

public, that it was very precious. She told me that she was only wearing it to wind Greville up."

"The Italian jewellery?"

"Cecil brought it back. He never would say how he got it. I think he must have stolen it from a church or something. He did tell me the whole set of that jewellery had a curse on it, and anyone who wore it. Look, Superintendent, he was my brother, and in his way, he was sometimes kind and generous to me and mine. He could be mean and spiteful, and his enemies were legion, but he did have a conscience if he felt he had done anyone an unforgivable wrong, and I was one of those. When my husband died, he took us all in, and although he was strict and dictatorial, he looked after us. He looked after Greville too. He was the eldest, and felt he had to. Yes, he had a mean streak, but sometimes, if he admired someone, or respected them, he would help, in his own way. This family meeting was all about that. He wanted all of the children to stand on their own two feet. He saw that by paying for everything, they were learning nothing. Yes, he usually went the wrong way about things, but I did care for him, and I miss him. I didn't kill him, or any of the others, and I don't know who did. I'm also very frightened. Whoever is killing us may not have finished."

"Then tell us what you know. Did you buy Ruby a drink last night?"

"Yes, I did, a double gin and tonic. It was quite early in the evening, and she put it on the table in front of her, and said she would drink it later. Just before I went to bed, I went to the Ladies with her. We were talking in there. She seemed very on the ball, quite talkative, mainly saying catty things about Greville. I did see that my drink, and several others, had not been touched, but when I went upstairs, I said good night, and she was drinking from the glass then."

"So the drink you bought her, and others, were sitting on the table for some time. Did you see anyone putting anything in them or fiddling with them?"

"No, but when we went to the loo, there were several of the family sitting at the table, and Oliver and Bill, and I think, Ted."

"Where were Wilfred and Percy?"

"Either playing pool or watching the football on the television in the pool room. I didn't see either of them go near Ruby."

"Do you know, or have ever heard of an Oswald John Waddington?"

"No, I don't think so. No, I'm sure I haven't. Why?"

"Because he has been present here in the pub for some time."

"It must be one of the staff then. No, it means nothing to me."

"Then, for the moment, you are free to go. There will be an officer present in the pub at all times. If you are worried, seek them out."

Saul waited until Julia had been shown out of the room, and then he called in Celia, Mo, and the supervisory officers on his team. Over a coffee he told them, "Well done for finding that knife in the waste bin, and thank you for all the information you and the team have amassed. Now, I have a lot more information. Ruby Greywell was drugged before she was knifed, quite professionally, in the back of the neck. It was the date rape drug, Rohipnal. I expect it was in one of the drinks. As you know it works quite rapidly, so it would have been taken late on in the evening. The pathologist tells me that the knife used on Ruby was not the one used on Cecil, which she suspects was a scalpel. We need to find that."

"I think we have sir. We finally got to search in the box room at the end of the yard. It was very carefully hidden at the back of the room where we found a loose brick and it was behind that. It has been bagged, and is secure."

"Well done. Let's hope it has some prints. The other knife had been wiped. All the prints we have taken here have been put up against this mystery set of prints,"

"The ones we found on the writing table, and the ones in the settle?"

"Yes the prints of a convicted con merchant, who uses the name of Oswald John Waddington. As the initials are those of Windle, I expect that is who he is. I want him watched, carefully."

"Consider it done sir. We have got all the family together, except for the woman in the cells, and Greville, of course, like you asked."

"Then I had better go and speak to the obnoxious lot of them, once I have done, we need to protect Brenda Royce, because if this is about money, she will be in grave danger. Has Tatum called in regularly?"

"Yes. We also found a little house to let, opposite her house, and have the keys from the agent, and the use of it. The heating is already on there, to stop the pipes freezing, and there is a back entrance. I have DC Noble in there now. Tatum said they have had a couple of visitors, and she wants to talk to you, sir, says there is something a little odd."

"She is a very bright young woman. As soon as I have finished talking to the family, I'll go round there. Mo, I'd like you to accompany me. Civilian clothes, please."

Chapter Thirteen

The group was sitting sullenly, in silence, when Saul went into the main bar. He looked at them, and said, "I have here a copy of the most recent will that was made by Cecil Greywell. I think the time has come to tell you what it says. This gentleman is the solicitor who drew it up, and he assures me it is legal, and will stand up to any challenge made. I have asked him to read it to you. Once you know where you all stand, then maybe these murders might just stop. Mr Morrissey, would you mind?"

"Yes, of course. Major Greywell came to me, and over a couple of days he drew up this will, and it was signed and witnessed the day before he was killed. I don't know any of you personally, so I think it best if I just read it. Please, don't interrupt, if you have any questions leave them to the end."

"I understood he had a will at his solicitors in York. He made it very recently."

"That is correct, Mr?"

"Windle, I was his business advisor."

"Yes, I have spoken to them, and they faxed me a copy of it. He revoked it, in this document. After the usual declaration of his doing so and being of sound mind, and arranging his funeral and that, this is what the main part says:-

To my brother Greville, I leave the Italian jewellery which he has coveted for so long, in the knowledge that he can never sell it. To his wife, Ruby, I leave nothing. To their daughters Melanie and Samantha, I leave one thousand pounds each.

To my sister Julia, I leave my main residence in York, in trust, and a fund from which the money will be available to pay for its upkeep for as long as she wishes to reside there. Should she marry, or wish to leave the house, it is to be sold and the money from the sale will be divided between her three children, Edward Arbuthnot, Alana Arbuthnot, and Wilfred Arbuthnot. The trustees will be Oliver Windle and my York solicitor, Graham Coddlestone or his appointed successor.

To Edward Arbuthnot, I leave ten thousand pounds. To Alana Arbuthnot I leave ten thousand pounds. To Wilfred Arbuthnot I leave twenty thousand pounds and my flat in Kensington.

To my son Percy, I leave fifty thousand pounds, and my house in Edinburgh.

To William Jones, my faithful friend and protector, I leave one hundred thousand pounds and my Bentley.

The remainder of my estate, including my other properties, my stocks and shares, and all the remaining monies and securities, after death duties and expenses and fees, I leave to my natural daughter, Brenda Doreen Royce, of 18 Bowskills Yard, Settle, without any restrictions for her to dispose of or use as she wishes. I believe her to be the most honest and industrious of all my relatives.

Should she predecease me, the property will be sold and the money divided between all the above beneficiaries."

There was a stunned silence. Mr Morrissey said, "As I understand it, having consulted with Major Greywell's solicitor in York, the rest of the estate bequeathed to Brenda Royce amounts to several million pounds in monies, and several houses and some industrial premises. Any questions?"

"Can we challenge it?" asked Julia.

"You can try, Mrs Arbuthnot, but I think it is pretty bomb-proof."

"How dare he," said Wilfred "leaving it all to a total stranger; hang on, that is the cleaner here, isn't it?"

"Yes, Wilfred it is," interjected Percy. "Even I could see the relationship, when I saw her. It was like looking in a mirror, and you know it. She is welcome to it, at least he didn't stop me marrying who I want. Hell, you got enough, didn't you?"

"No, Percy, I didn't. I was his son, damn it, he owed me more than that."

"Before you all start picking over the details with Mr Morrissey here," said Saul "let me warn all of you, there is a murderer amongst you. Don't trust anyone. I have other things to do, so I will leave you with my officers here. Good evening."

Saul sighed with relief when he walked out of the pub. On the pavement, he bumped into his son, Sam.

"Hello, Dad! You still busy?"

"Yes, what are you up to?"

"I went for a very snowy walk, had a pub lunch at the Royal Oak, and then I met some chaps here from the Cave Rescue, and they asked me if I wanted to join them tomorrow for a trip up Whernside, and I said I'd let them know. I heard something too, you might want to know about."

"What?"

"It is about the local dentist. Thought it a bit odd. Everyone agrees he's an excellent dentist, but they were talking about when he first came here, years ago. One chap reckons he was quite rich, he set up the surgery, real posh it is, and then he didn't pay the workmen, not for ages. Suddenly he came into lots of money again, and things settled down. Some like him, quite a few don't. They say he spends a lot of money. Did you know he has four cars, well three, and a Land Rover? They were saying you can tell his Land Rover, it is the only one round here that is bright turquoise."

"Thank you. Have you rung your mother today?"

"Yes, I did. She said you had rung, and that Auntie Ruth arrives tomorrow. She told me that I should get back, that I should be working at home, not gallivanting around here, getting in your way. I said I'd come home when I was able, and not before you said I had to. I can stay here for a day or so, please, Dad?"

"Coward! Yes, of course you can. When I rang your mother, I told her that you were being very useful, and she shut up about it. Sam, have you found a laundrette here?"

"Yes, I know where it is. Where is your washing?"

"In my case. I expect you have some too. Would you see to it?"

"Sure."

Saul's mobile phone rang, and he answered it. He listened for some time, and then said, "Right, bring him in, and question him about it. I am going to see young Brenda Royce."

He said goodbye to his son and walked up the street, where he met Mo. Together they walked the short distance to Brenda's house and knocked on the door. It was answered by Tatum, who looked carefully through the chink in the chained door, before letting them in. Brenda was sitting with two cats on her lap, watching the television, which she turned off, and was about to get up, when Saul said, "No, please don't get up. How are you?"

"Nervous, worried, but I've got over the shock of it all, I think. I admit, it did shake me up quite a bit, but I didn't care for him, so it doesn't hurt that much. Do you really think I'm in danger?"

"I don't know, but you could be. Are you happy with Tatum here?"

"Yes, we get on well. She is very discreet. Not in the way at all. Actually, we are having quite a bit of fun. Do sit down, shall I make you a cup of coffee?"

"I'd love one, yes, but I expect Tatum could do it. I need to talk to you again."

Mo said, "I'll go into the kitchen with Tatum, while you talk, sir."

Saul sat down in an old, but very comfy leather armchair. He looked round the small living room, and saw that it was decorated with taste and simplicity. He saw a display cabinet with many trophies. Beside Brenda was a complex piece of embroidery, half done.

"What are all these trophies for?"

"Sport, running, hockey, tennis, and orienteering. There are a couple for swimming as well. I like sport, a lot."

"And you are very good at it, obviously. Have you had any visitors today?"

"Yes, my mum came round this morning, and then later this afternoon, my stepdad came. They seem to be worried about me. My stepdad said you were frightening me, he thought unnecessarily. Oh, yes, Dr Lewis popped in at lunchtime, just to

163

see I was OK. He delivered me, I've known him all my life. He said that if you thought I needed protection, then I should accept it. He said if I wanted to talk to him at any time, I could. I don't know why, but he and my stepdad have never really got on."

"Is there anything you need?"

"Not really, no. We went shopping in the Co-op earlier, and got everything. Elaine popped in, too, on her way back from shopping. I have an appointment tomorrow morning, with the solicitor, ten o'clock."

"Mr Morrissey? May I ask what for?"

"I think I need to make a will. All this sudden death has got me thinking. If I am to have money, I must make sure everything is sorted, just in case."

"Very sensible, but what made you think of it?"

"Just something my stepdad said. Quite how he knew I was due to come into money, I'm not sure, because I never told him, but it does make sense."

"I see. Look, young lady, just be very careful, will you? Who had you intended to leave your wealth to?"

"I was going to leave it to my mum, but Dad said it might be better to set up a trust fund for the boys. He offered to be a trustee. He always has dealt with the family finances. I was also going to leave some money to one or two friends. I have no intention of being knocked off for a very long time, but he said it was better to cover everything. I know he was only looking out for my best interests, but it scared me a bit. I talked it over with Tatum, and she said I should tell you. Thanks for coming round."

"Would you rather go away for a few days? I can get someone to look after the cats."

"Not really, no. At least I know where I am here."

Mo and Tatum arrived with the coffee, and the conversation became more general, mainly about the weather. After half an hour, Saul said, "Thank you for your hospitality, Brenda. I need to brief Tatum for a few minutes, so Mo will stop with you until she gets back, is that all right?"

"Fine. Mo and I have known each other a long time. Mo, can you help me with changing the light bulb in the kitchen?"

Tatum walked down to the Talbot Arms with Saul. As they walked, he said, "Wait until we are sitting down. Then tell me what is worrying you."

Over a pint of lager, Saul found a quiet corner of the bar, and asked, "What worried you?"

"I know it sounds daft sir, but it was her stepfather, Mr Royce. He wasn't pleased to see me there, at all. He intended to scare her, and she had a reserve about her when he was there. She was uneasy. He almost railroaded her into making a will, and virtually suggested she leave everything to him, or as a trustee to him for her family. He kept saying it was important, and urgent. Then, later, he said he was planning a walk up a local beauty spot here, in the snow, and asked her to go with him. It is over at Malham. I know that area, and it is quite dangerous in this weather. He said it might relax her, to get away from it all. She said I'd have to go too, and I wasn't keen on the idea."

"Why? I am sure you could manage a winter walk."

"That's just it, sir, she knows me well enough to know I would love it. I do a lot of walking. I'm even on the Cave Rescue. She didn't want to go with him. I may be wrong, but I think she is frightened of him. There is something, an undercurrent of some importance, there. She tells me how much she loves and admires him, but something is worrying her, about him. After he left, she was very quiet for a while, and then I asked her why she didn't want to go for a walk with him. She said, 'I'm sorry, I shouldn't have used you like that, I just don't fancy it. I know you would be fine with a walk like that, but Mr Catchpole told me to trust nobody, so I'm doing what he said.' I thought I should tell you sir, I'm sorry if I wasted your time. I know you are busy."

"No, you haven't. Well done, officer, I am very pleased with you. You have great observation and a sensible head on your shoulders. Did you see if anyone was hanging around today, anyone unusual?"

"Yes, indeed I did. Someone has moved into the place opposite, no luggage to speak of, and Brenda said there were some strangers around. One of them was that fat man from the hotel, the one that whispers. He looked as if he was just out walking, but his footwear was wrong. Brenda said he gave her the creeps. When we were shopping, in the square, I saw him down by the chemists, and he was talking to Mr Royce. When we came out of the shop we were coming straight back here, and he began to follow us, at a distance, not obviously, so I pulled Brenda into the café, and we had a cup of tea and a butty, and I made sure he had gone before we came out. Then we went round the long way, past the drapers. I've put everyone and everything I saw and heard in my report. I gave it to Mo in the kitchen just now."

"Thank you. The people opposite are our chaps. Now, are you happy to continue?"

"If that is how I can be of use, sure."

"Then I have an attack bleeper, if you need it. Press this, and we will come running. If you are at all worried, I need to know straight away. Ring me, if you can, on my mobile number."

"I don't want to cause a false alarm."

"I don't care if there are a few false alarms, if you think anything is odd, ring me, and if you are worried, press this. Don't let her out of your sight. If she wants to go to work, go with her, and help her. If she wants to go for a walk, then ring me, and I will get someone to go with you. Actually, my son, who's staying in town, might be the very person. I know he will protect you."

"Yes, he called in the station when I was in there. He's fun! I was chatting to him. He asked me out on a date, do you mind?"

"Did he? No wonder he wants to hang around here. The sly bugger! No, I don't mind. Are you interested? Do you have a boyfriend, tell me to mind my own business if you want?"

"No, I don't and I was very flattered. He's ever so good looking. He said he likes sport, like me and Brenda. He doesn't have a girlfriend, does he, he's not just amusing himself?"

"Oh, yes, he is, but no, I'm not aware of any lady friend. He's a genuine lad. He is also rather sensitive, please don't break his heart. I have enough family troubles already."

"Do you? It had never occurred to me that you would have anything but a well ordered life. You're so organised. I'm sorry, I shouldn't pry. I was taking a liberty."

"No, it's all right. You have a very healthy curiosity, signs of a good detective. Just keep it to yourself, please."

"Can I help?"

"Bless you, child, no, but thanks for the offer. Yes, you can, keep him out of trouble. Now, if it's all right with you, I'll take you back to Brenda, and then you get to bed. Lock the doors, and sleep light. I doubt anything will happen until this will is signed, but be watchful. Be over cautious, and if Brenda wants to talk, listen. There is something she isn't telling us."

As Saul and Mo walked down the snowy street together, Mo said, "You think someone is going to try and kill her, don't you?"

"I'm afraid so. I may be wrong, but I don't think I am. I know a lot more now, and by tomorrow, I think I will have enough to make at least one arrest. They have pulled Windle in, mainly to identify him. Tell me about Royce."

"Good dentist, but he has many fingers in many pies. He also owns a couple of farms round here, with tenants. Both of them, funnily enough, ones that Greywell got many years ago."

"And he has a turquoise Land Rover. I think I need to see this Mr Royce, but it's too late now. I'll call on him in the morning. I'm knackered, and I expect you are too. I'll sort out what is needed at the nick, and then I'll get off to my lodgings. It will be a busy day tomorrow."

"I'll be there. Have you eaten tonight?"

"No, I'll have a sandwich when I get in."

"If you want, I've a good Lancashire hotpot at home, in the slow cooker, and a passable bottle of wine, if you would like to join me you would be very welcome. I'm only round the corner from you."

"You have? If you are sure, I don't want to impose."

"No, I'd be grateful of the company. I'll hang on at the nick, and we can walk home together."

At the police station they both sifted through the messages, and Saul went down to the cell block. Sgt Graves was on duty.

"Oh, sir, I was about to page you. Windle has finally admitted to having that other name, and your skipper said he has got nothing more out of him. Greville Greywell has been bailed, and so has his daughter. Archie Babble got arrested for being drunk, again, and is in custody. That is him you can hear trying to sing in the cells now. The patrols are already out. Can I do anything more?"

"Yes, tell me how many turquoise Land Rovers are to be found round here?"

"Only the one that I know of. Mr Royce's. Did I mention I saw him in the Golden Lion last week? I thought he had popped in to see Brenda, but she wasn't on duty. Are you interested in him?"

"Yes. Do you know anything about him?"

"Not a lot. He is a good dentist. He was banned for drink-driving several years ago, for a year, his wife drove him round. He owns a bit of property round here. I heard a strange story about him, years ago, when he first came here. I have no idea if it is true. Apparently, he was an army dentist originally. He had a practice somewhere down south, sold up suddenly and came up here. I do know that he has at least one business partner, sleeping ones."

"How do you know that?"

"My dad told me. Royce arrived here just as Dad retired. I'll give you my dad's number. Give him a ring tomorrow."

"I will. If there is anything urgent, ring me on my mobile. I'm going round to Mo's for a meal, and then back to my digs. I'll be in early. Goodnight!"

Saul had a very pleasant hour at Mo's, the food was excellent, the wine better and the company amusing. He got back to his lodgings and expected everyone to be in bed, but

Sam was talking to Chris and Lynn, in the lounge. They got up, and Chris said, "At last, we meet our important guest. Have you eaten? If not, it won't take long to cook something."

"Thank you, I have eaten. I trust I am not putting you out?"

"No, and your lad, young Sam, here has made himself useful. He has been helping Chris with chopping logs, and with tidying the garage. My grandchildren were round earlier, and they think he is wonderful, because he played a game with them. Do you need anything?"

"Is it all right if I have a bath? I will be out early, could you put out some bread for me to have for breakfast?"

"Fine, I've laid up, and everything is there. Oh, and your wife phoned and left a message. I've written it down for you, and left it in your room. I found Sam heading off to the laundrette earlier, so I stopped him and your washing is now airing in the airing cupboard, and will be ready tomorrow."

After a brief chat with Sam, Saul made it to bed, and slept well, until his alarm woke him.

Chapter Fourteen

Diana picked up her elder sister Ruth from the station. Whilst she was delighted to see her, she was apprehensive about her visit. Every time Ruth descended on them, she found fault with almost everything in the house, and was always critical of Saul, the household arrangements, and over the last few months she had been very scathing about Sam, as she had been about his elder brother Stephen.

Diana was very proud of all her children. She loved Saul very much, and his tolerance, patience and gentleness had never wavered. She had seen him lose his temper, but never with her, or his children. His main fault that she could identify was that he was too placid, too polite, and if he didn't like someone or something he would withdraw into his shell, and become so icily polite it was almost embarrassing.

When Ruth moaned about the snow-covered roads, and then scathingly intimated that Diana should have called Sam back to the house to clear the paths in the garden, Diana became rather annoyed. She had been rather upset when Sam had chosen to stay away from his home in order to avoid Ruth, and, she suspected, her. Ruth was no sooner in the house than she criticised the washing up being left in the sink. Then it was the position of the furniture in the lounge. She and Saul had bought the new suite, and had carefully selected it to go just there. Next it was the decoration in the spare bedroom.

"Diana, dear, this shade of peach is just ghastly. It is neither one thing nor the other. Wishy-washy. I can't possibly sleep in here, I'll take Sam's room instead. He can move into here. Why isn't he working, if he isn't here to help around the house?"

"He is spending time with his father. He has been studying really hard at college, for an extra two scholarships. This is his holiday, and if he wants to spend it with Saul, then I think he should. I'm sorry, but his room is his, and he has all his stuff in there. I have no intention of booting him out. I like the colour in here, and so does Saul. We chose it together, and decorated it ourselves."

"You mean he chose it and got you to do the work. No, dear, I'll take Sam's room. He can move his stuff back in."

"No, Ruth, he won't. His computer and all his books are there, not to mention his clothes. He hates anyone else in his room, so you can stay in here and like it."

"I suppose that odious husband of yours has been allowing you to be dictated to again. Whose house is this, anyway? Yours or your son's?"

"Actually, it belongs to Saul and me. Not you, not the children. As Saul paid for most of it, I suggest you argue with him, not me."

"I will. When is he due back from his latest jaunt?"

"When he is ready. Ruth, let's not fall out. Come and have a cup of something, and tell me all your news."

"Oh, very well. Quite why you have stayed with that boring man, I'll never know. You could have done much better for yourself, you know."

"I don't think we have done badly, and I happen to love him."

"Well I'm sure you think you do, but he is so deadly dull!"

"I doubt all the murderers he catches think that, or the other criminals he locks up. He isn't dull, actually, just very gentle."

"If you say so, dear."

As they sat in the lounge over a cup of tea, Diana watched her sister looking at everything in the room, with apparent distaste. Ruth's eyes fell on a large watercolour, of moors, heather and mountains, which was a new addition.

"That's new, it's rather good actually. I'm surprised, you don't normally buy that kind of picture. How much did you give for it?"

"It was given by the artist. I like it, too."

"Is it someone I might have heard of?"

"Oh, yes, you have. Saul painted it last year, when he was out walking. He is a very clever artist you know."

Ruth made a sort of snorting noise, and changed the subject quickly, to that of the two girls' education.

"What is this nonsense about them going to a different school?"

"Saul and I have discussed it, and we have decided it would be the best thing for them."

"If that is your decision, then I shall not be helping you pay for them. I don't think it is at all a good idea."

"Thank you, but we don't need any financial help, Ruth. It was kind of you to think of it, but we think it is for the best, for both of them. Thank you ever so much for the postcards from North Africa, did you have a good time?"

"Not too bad. Camping in the desert is an invigorating experience; the man in charge was a bit of a male chauvinist bigot, but it was very interesting, the ancient cultures the ruins and the wildlife. I've brought the video I took, we can watch it tonight if you like."

"I'm sure Saul and Sam would love to see it too. Can we wait until they are home?"

"If you like. Why is Sam going with Saul on a case?"

"I'm not sure. He said he wanted to do some thinking, and suggested his father could help him."

"I doubt it, but I suppose he has to play these games. He'll grow up one day, I suppose."

As the day wore on, Diana became very irritated. She saw her sister in a new light. When the girls came in, Ruth became charming, and almost complimentary about them. Ruth asked for, and was given help putting presents under the tree, which was then completely redecorated. She noticed that there were presents for her and the girls, but none for Saul or Sam. After the girls had gone upstairs, she said, "The men will be back for Christmas, I'm sure. Do you want to put their presents there now?"

"I haven't bothered with any. I'm sure they don't have any need for more socks or aftershave. I concentrated on the girls."

"Oh, I see. Never mind. Why do you hate the men in my family, Ruth?"

"I don't, it is just I don't have much respect for many men. Why should I love the man who stole you from me? You and I used to be so close. You depended on me for everything. I thought I still mattered to you. If you pamper and fuss any man, he gets big-headed and selfish. Our mother made that mistake. Look how awful Dad was to us, after she left."

"She had cancer, she died."

"Yes, after she left him. He caused the whole thing, I never told you all this, but if he hadn't been so demanding, she would never have got so ill in the first place. Of course, he felt guilty when he realised what he had done. He wasn't man enough to admit it, and that is why he had the accident that killed him, he was wallowing in self-pity, and lost concentration."

"That is a horrid thing to say, Ruth. You always told me it was an accident. Now you are insinuating it was almost suicide. How could he have caused Mum to have cancer?"

"Because he wasn't a very nice man, and he ran her ragged. You were not old enough to understand. You had to be protected from it all. I am not going to let you be killed by any man. Saul uses you, badly. He expects you to work, and four children are far too many. You run the house, what does he do, but go swanning off to be the big important detective. Open your eyes, woman, he treats you like dirt!"

"No, he doesn't! It was my desire to return to work, he never asked me to. I wanted more children, as much as he did. If I wanted to, I could give up work entirely, but I need to keep my mind alert."

"Then do another degree, or something."

"Please stop trying to come between Saul and me. I have everything I need, and most of what I want. Despite what you think, Ruth, he is a good man, and he loves me. Yes, he works long hours away, sometimes, but we have wonderful holidays, and a good life."

"I had always hoped you would be more than just a housewife. You could have been a head teacher at least by now, or even a university don. You were doing so well, and then you met him, and you gave it all up."

"Yes, I did, but I don't regret it. I have four wonderful children, and a comfortable home, and I doubt I shall ever want for anything."

"I hardly call Stephen a wonderful child. He has left, when did you last see him?"

"Not long ago. He is doing well. He is now a grown man, and I cannot hang on to him for ever. There comes a time when you have to let them cut the apron strings. That is something you were never able to do with me, Ruth. I appreciate your support and love, always have done, but I must be allowed to live my life as I want, not you."

"You never did understand what was important in life. I failed to teach you that. I blame myself. See him for what he is: a sullen, self-indulgent man, who is quite happy for you to be the little woman at home, overshadowed by his pompous self-importance."

Diana changed the subject again, but all day she was thinking about what had been said. Ruth's advice to open her eyes had been good, but not in the way Ruth had intended. She considered how she had treated Sam over the last few weeks. She realised with a growing chilling horror how distant Saul had been for the last few months. She needed time to think, away from both Ruth and her family. Suddenly, she needed to talk to Saul, face to face. Ruth had announced she was going to take the girls out for a walk, and then to the cinema. Diana asked, "I've been thinking about what you said, Ruth. I need to go away and think things through, could you hold the fort here for a couple of days? Would you mind looking after the girls? I know they would love it."

"What a wonderful idea. I hope it works and you come to your senses. Where are you going?"

"I'm not sure. I'll have the mobile with me, and I'll take my car. I'll probably go to some friends in Wakefield."

Diana felt dreadful at her duplicity, but she needed to escape Ruth, and she knew the girls would be safe. As she got into the car, she checked she had all she needed, and drove to the station. On the platform, she rang Saul.

"Hello, it's me. Look, I desperately need to be with you, just for a while. Are you very busy? Thank you, can I stay where you are, is there room? I gather that the roads are blocked, but the trains are getting through. What is the address? We need to talk urgently, Sam too."

Saul, who had been in a meeting with his team, walked slowly back into the room, very thoughtful. He was worried that all was not well. He wondered if she was going to ask for a divorce or separation. He found it difficult to concentrate. The case was progressing. He had already opened the inquests into the deaths at the Town Hall, and had applied for and obtained several search warrants, some of which had already been executed in various parts of the country. He had arranged for Greville's house and business, and bank records to be searched, and Windle's. He was wondering whether to use the last warrant up, or keep it, when he was called to the front office.

Brenda and Tatum were there, and asked to talk to him. With them was Sam. He raised an eyebrow in surprise.

"Mr Catchpole, can I talk to you again, please? Tatum and I went out for a walk, and Sam here came with us. Sam says that you will understand, and Tatum has always said I must tell you everything. You knew I was holding something back, didn't you?"

"That it was your stepfather you saw walking home in the middle of the night that Major Greywell was killed, yes."

"You knew, how?"

"It has been worrying you, I know. What else do you want to tell me? I promise to listen, without criticising."

"Sam said you would. Can I talk to you alone?"

"If you wish. You two, go and get a coffee, have a break or something. Come back in an hour or so, I'll look after young Brenda here."

In his office, he pulled up a chair for Brenda, and ushered her into it. He made a coffee for both of them and sat down, and said, "Tell me, it's worrying you to the point of distraction, I know, and now it is frightening you."

"I don't want to get anyone into trouble, and I may have it all wrong."

"That is always possible, I grant you. Let me make the difficult decisions. It's my job."

"OK. Yes, it was my stepfather I saw. When I asked him if he had been out that night, he said he hadn't, but he had, because I asked my mother, and she said he had been out most of the night. He took the Land Rover, and told her he was checking stock, which he never does. He just lets the farms out, never does any actual farming. It has been worrying me about why he lied. There are one or two other things I am confused about, too."

"Go on. There may be a quite innocent explanation for all this."

"Well, no, I don't think so. Dad was always a keen photographer, used to take snaps of all of us, all the time. Just after he married Mum, he took several of me, at the beach. I had a real nice swimming costume, new it was, with a pattern of fish on it. I only wore it on that holiday, and it got torn on the last day there, so we threw it away before we came home. Then there was the time, several years later, when I had my hair really long, and a shocking pink T-shirt, again with a pattern, this time of stars and shells. I know, red hair, pink top, doesn't go, but I liked it. He took another photo, and my mum said it was dreadful and she threw it away. Then when I won one of my running medals, he took another, at the stadium. He said he had lost it, and the second one hadn't come out. Now, I remember, I turned the medal round for the second picture. He only ever took one of the boys, but always two of me. There were quite a few of me that never came out, so he said."

Saul waited patiently.

"When I was cleaning Major Greywell's room, there were lots of papers neatly stacked on his table. I knocked one file of them off, and amongst all sorts of things that dropped on the floor, there were some photos. I remember looking at them and thinking he must have had a daughter with the same taste and the same clothes, until it sunk in that these pictures were of me, which my stepfather had said had never come out. I tidied them up, as best I could, and even apologised to Major Greywell for disturbing his files. He was quite charming about it. I was thinking about it for the rest of the day. If, as he said, he didn't know about me, then how did he get them, and why would he have them? Why did my stepfather lie? Then before I found Major Greywell, I cleaned his room, and I can tell you for certain, that file was missing. I know, because I looked for it, I was going to try and sneak a second look. I shouldn't have, but it was important to me. Have you found them?"

"No. There is more, go on, you are doing very well."

"How did my stepfather know that Major Greywell was going to leave me any money? He did, and I never told him, did you?"

"No, nor did any of my officers."

"When Mum came round yesterday, Dad didn't know about it, but we had quite a talk. Something is troubling her, and she told me that my stepfather is not the wonderful person I thought him to be. She said she wondered if she should talk to you. I think she suspects him of something bad, but she doesn't know what to do. I love her very much, and I am afraid she might be in danger if I don't tell someone all this. He asked her to give him an alibi, that night. She said she didn't know what she would say if you asked her. I think she is very afraid of telling you he was out that night. When I asked him if he had gone out for a walk that night, he gave me a very odd look, told me I was being silly. I caught him looking at me later, in a very odd way. It was like there was a different person behind the eyes. I'm not explaining this very well, am I? It sounds like fanciful gibberish."

"Brenda, you are one of the most observant and intelligent people I have met in quite a while. It isn't gibberish at all. I understand just what you are telling me. If you were not about to become a rich heiress, I'd encourage you to think of becoming a detective, at least a police officer."

"Funny you should say that, I wanted to, about five years ago, but my stepfather was so against it, he made Mum ask me not to. She told me that he was so upset about it, that it would turn him against me. It was then, when I said I wouldn't, that he and Mum gave me the house. He insisted the house was put in his name, he said for legal reasons, as I wasn't yet twenty-one. Last year, I had quite a bit of money saved, and asked him if I could sell it and get a bigger place and he refused. Said it was daft. That was one of the few fallings out we had. He wouldn't sign it over to me, at all, even though they always said it was my money that they bought it with. He says there is a trust fund for me, that he controls, that I shall get when I am thirty, but I have always been a bit scared of pushing it. He said he had invested the money for me, and gives me an allowance, but he has to handle it, so I don't pay too much tax."

"What are you actually frightened of?"

"I've been thinking back, about him. He has always been very kind, in his way, but he is a control freak. I'm not sure my mother is all that happy. Mum said he turned up after I had been born, and for ages she didn't want to know. She turned him down several times, you know. She told me yesterday that he has never been faithful to her, but always he has had such a hold over the finances that she couldn't afford to divorce him. She told me this yesterday, I had no idea. What is going on? He looked at me yesterday, and I saw a stranger, it was almost as if he was thinking of getting rid of me. For almost the first time, I have struck out on my own, and he is trying to control me. I had a boyfriend last year, nice lad, Nathan. Dad was very against him, and suddenly Nathan got offered a job down south. He wanted to marry me, but Dad said something to him that put him off. That made me see that Nathan wasn't the person I thought he was, but I did wonder."

"Did you make your will, like he asked, this morning?"

"Yes, and no. Yes, I made a will, but I left everything to my younger brothers, not him or Mum. I asked the solicitor to be an executor, and trustee, and I also asked Dr Lewis to be a trustee. What made me come to you, is that Dad rang the solicitor while I was there, and said he would come in and check the will. Mr Morrissey told me to come to you. He suggested that we tell Dad that the will has been made, and he is the beneficiary, but really, he isn't, just to get him off my back. I signed the will this morning. Mr Morrissey says he needs to see you about it, that there is something very strange. He says he knows nothing about the trust fund, and I showed him what documents I have for the house, and he says Dad could sell the house without my say so, if he wanted to. You think my stepdad is the killer, don't you? Because I do."

"I'm sorry, Brenda, but I think he could be, at least involved. I'll get you out of here as soon as I can, where he can't get to you."

"No, if I do that, he will only make my mother suffer. I need to know, you see. If he is, once he thinks I have made my will in his favour, I think I will meet with a fatal accident, except you are one step ahead of him. I wouldn't mind, but he has a set of keys to my house, you know, said he needed them, just in case."

"My dear child, you cannot put yourself up as bait, I won't allow it. These killers are dangerous, very dangerous. I have here a search warrant, for his house and all his premises. You have given me as much information as I need to execute it. I want you to stay here, I am going to get Mr Morrissey over here. If you are prepared to help me, then maybe we can resolve this."

"Can you also protect my mother?"

"I'll do my best."

Saul called in one of his sergeants, and said, "Miss Royce is going to give a statement. I should be back by the time she has finished, but stay with her, and keep her safe, please. Have you had something to eat, Brenda?"

"No, but I'm not that hungry."

"Feed her, and protect her with all your ability. Don't worry, lass, we'll keep you and your mother safe. Skipper, call in all the troops apart from those on observation duty. I need to do a search. Young Tatum should be on her mobile, get her and that lad of mine back here, please. We need to act fast."

Saul almost ran across the road to the solicitors, and was shown straight in. Twenty minutes later he returned to the police station with Morrissey, and his secretary. They retreated to an office with Brenda, and then Saul came out, and said, "Mo, stay here with Brenda and Mr Morrissey. Tatum, would you go to Brenda's house, and stay there. Sam, if you want to, go with her. The rest of you, including uniform, we want to search these premises, on this list. Come on, we cannot waste any time. If anyone sees either Greville Greywell, Tim Royce, or Oliver Windle, tell me."

Saul went straight to the dental surgery with several officers, while Celia lead a team to Royce's home. The only person in the surgery was the dental nurse, who regarded him suspiciously.

"Mr Royce has closed the surgery for the afternoon. I'm just about to leave. What do you have to see him about?"

"I have a warrant to search these premises. Do you know where he is?"

"No, he asked me to cancel the few appointments this afternoon, and said he would be back on Monday. What on earth is going on? I'll try his mobile."

"Please do. Have you keys for everything?"

"Everything but the safe, yes. Here, take them. What are you looking for? This must be a mistake. Is it something to do with that man that was murdered, that was going to leave his money to his illegitimate daughter?"

"How do you know about that?"

"I overheard him. I know something is wrong, have done since then. I got the impression it was all an act, I think for my benefit. They obviously knew each other, and Tim made out he had to mend the dentures, but they were fine, just needed checking. Why Tim needed to take a series of impressions of them, I don't know, but he said he would do them later, after I had gone. I know he locked it all in the safe."

The search of the premises turned up a number of interesting items. Hidden in a cupboard, they found a set of keys, one of which opened the safe. While the items were bagged, Saul looked at a key in the safe, and compared it with the one he had been given for the back door of the Hotel. It matched. He also found an impression of some other keys, in a tin. He looked at some of the newer keys on the ring. They had been rather crudely made from the impressions. He paused, and thought about the keys they had found in Major Greywell's room. Celia rang him, and said that Doreen Royce was being very co-operative, but that Royce was out, and was not answering his mobile. While one of his officers took a statement from the dental nurse, who apparently had little love for Royce, the team cleared up, and Saul took a call from Morrissey.

Saul left the team to finish, and went back to the station. He was checking several messages, when Tatum rang and told him that she had seen Royce, Windle and Greville walking together past Brenda's house. They had barely glanced at the house, and had disappeared up towards the walk on Castleberg Crag, above the town. Simultaneously, Mo came in with messages from the other officers watching the house and other suspects, telling him the same.

Saul called in all the officers he could find, and with Mo, briefed them to cover every exit to the walk, and sent them off to get into position.

"We have sufficient evidence to arrest all three. I would rather do it without any hassle, but I think they are getting desperate. Watch, and wait. Try not to show yourself. Channel nineteen on the radio, please. I shall be Mike Tango one five, and Celia will be one six. The rest of you have your call signs."

As they went out to the back yard, Brenda ran out, with Mo in hot pursuit, and grabbed hold of Saul's arm.

"Are my mother and brothers all right?"

"Yes, they are. They are coming here to the station. Officers are with them. Please, go back and wait with them."

"No. If he is going to try to kill me, then it will show him for what he is. I want to come with you, please."

"So he can kill you, no dear, I have to protect you, it will make things much harder if you are there. He did call in at the solicitors this morning and was shown the will you wanted him to see, not the real one. He thinks he can get away with it. The front of your house can be seen from where he is now. I cannot put you at risk."

"Well I can. Why don't I go into my house, and then leave by climbing out of the back window, over Mrs Twinning's wall, and then back here? That might draw him in, and you can catch him there. In the act, so to speak."

Saul looked down at her. That she was dreadfully distressed was obvious, but there was a tilt to her jaw that spoke of great determination. He thought about it, and said, "You can do that? Not be seen, with safety?"

"Yes, I can. It is the only fire exit, and she won't mind. I tried it once, just to check, and it is easy. You see, it would be easier for me to know for myself. That he wants to kill me, I mean. Then I promise, I'll come back here and stay with Mum, she'll need me, I think."

"You must do exactly as I say, at once?"

"Of course."

"Then put on this vest, under your coat. It's a stab-proof vest. Go straight in and out immediately. Whatever he says to you, know your family is safe. I expect he will ring you. I think you only have a mobile phone? Yes, he may suggest you meet him. Are you sure you want to do this?"

"Yes, I am."

"Frightened?"

"Very."

"And very brave. Now, go and get ready."

Saul made the necessary calls, and within ten minutes, Brenda walked at a normal pace from the main square, up the back streets to her house. Although she knew there were officers around, she saw no one. She couldn't resist a glance up at the imposing rocks of Castleberg above the town, but she could see no one through the trees. She got to the front door, and noticed a package on the doorstep, which she saw was from her stepfather. She gingerly picked it up, and took it inside, where she put it on the table in the small kitchen. Tatum and Sam were waiting for her.

"Right Brenda, Sam will go with you, get straight out of the back. You will meet an officer as soon as you are out, and he is coming in the same way, to be with me." Brenda nodded, and with Sam, headed up and out of her bathroom window. Sam helped her down, and into the arms of a waiting, rather robust officer in a civilian jacket, who Sam then helped pull up, before he slid down to join Brenda. He took her hand and they ran through the back street to work their way round the square, and got back to the police station.

The officer joined Tatum, and they waited silently in the kitchen, having sent a text to Saul that the house was prepared. They examined the package; it contained some very expensive Belgian chocolates, and a note from Royce that read:

'I thought you might like a bit of cheering up, after the awful time you have had. Treat yourself! Dad.'

They left it, opened but uneaten, having removed several chocolates, into an evidence bag which they took upstairs with them. They sent Saul a text to that effect, and his reply was:

WAIT

Brenda sat with Mo in the station. After about half an hour, her mobile went off, and she saw the call was from Royce. She answered it, rather drowsily.

"What are you doing up there? I'm ever so sleepy, Dad, I'd rather not. Why not come here? Oh, all right, I'll meet you there. Thanks for the chocolates, they were yummy."

More messages went back and forth. Before long Tatum, in Brenda's warm hooded coat, left the house, and headed down the road to the gates into the Castleberg walk, and there she met Saul. In the ice and snow he followed her up the zigzag pathway, as she slipped and tripped, as though she was stupefied. She was much the same height and build as Brenda, and the hood remained up, as she slowly climbed to the summit. Saul, although big, was also light on his feet, and followed under the cover of the snow-covered trees, always keeping her in sight. Tatum had almost got to the top, by the flag pole, when Royce came down the path to meet her. Saul saw him, from just below, and heard him say, "Whatever is the matter, dear? Come and sit down. You look drunk, are you?"

Only when Tatum was very close did he realise he had been fooled. She looked in his hand, and saw a syringe there, ready and filled with a clear liquid. She knew exactly what to do, and didn't hesitate, she turned and ran back down the path, past Saul, and other officers, into the waiting protection of some uniform officers, on a large green area. Saul filled the path in front of Royce, who skidded to a halt as he saw his quarry had escaped him. He turned to go back the other way, when he saw Oliver Windle backing up his part of the path, and beyond him some burly police officers.

"Timothy Royce, I am arresting you on suspicion of murder and attempted murder, now, be sensible, put that syringe down, and give yourself up. I am Superintendent Catchpole, and you really have nowhere left to go. I warn you, you do not have to say anything unless you wish to do so, but it may harm your defence if you fail to mention when questioned anything you later rely on in court. Anything you do say will be taken down and may be given in evidence."

Royce looked wildly around him. The cliff below him was vertical, and there was a wall behind him. Neither offered an easy way out. Behind him, Windle was blocking his way, and beyond him a posse of police. All that stood between him and liberty, so far as he could see, was a tall but slender middle-aged man. His decision made, he rushed Saul, and as they met, he tried to inject him, but the syringe flew out of his hand into the trees underneath them. They struggled on the narrow path, while officers ran up to assist Saul, but the space was too small. Royce was a big, heavy man. He knew he would soon be overpowered from behind, and grasping Saul's coat, he jumped over the cliff edge, pulling Saul with him as they fell, crashing through the trees, down the cliff face.

Windle gave himself up, and submitted to being handcuffed and led down the path. Officers rushed to where the two men had fallen. They fought their way through the undergrowth, and the snow, and several falling rocks that were cascading down the cliff face. Saul was clinging onto Royce with a desperate grip, from which Royce was unable to free himself. Royce and Saul rolled over and by the time other officers were there, they had come to a halt on a pathway. Royce was pulled off Saul, and Sergeant Graves took charge.

"Get an ambulance, quickly! You lot, look after him, and search him, in case he has anything else, weapon or whatever. Sir, can you hear me?"

"Mercifully, yes, but I think my leg is broken, and my head hurts like hell, my arm and ribs too. I'm not feeling too good, actually."

Saul was covered in blood, and had a deep gash on his scalp, and was bleeding from many cuts and abrasions. His left leg was at a strange angle, and his left arm was dangling in an unhealthy way. He lay, biting his lip, while he was made more comfortable. He looked over at Royce, who was also injured, but from the abuse and struggling, not so badly. Saul began to feel very cold, and muttered, "Too cold, Graves, Can't think straight."

"Don't worry, you'll be reet, sir. The ambulance is on its way. We have a stretcher, the paramedics are on the path now. We'll get you out by helicopter. It has been scrambled. Lie still. You will live, you know, we get much worse out of caves. I know, search for the syringe and other evidence. Keep talking to me."

"The other two, Greville and Windle?"

"Gave up, and are already in custody. It's a pity, but Royce seems to be going to live."

"Please don't put me in a bed next to him. Did you see it?"

"Yes, he deliberately pulled you off. We all saw it. Do you want anyone told?"

"My son, and my wife, please. Ouch, that hurts! Must you move me?"

"Sorry. Here are the medics. I'll come with you."

"Whatever. Is the WPc safe?"

"Yes, fine."

The paramedics quickly took over, and soon Saul was in less pain. With his good arm, he pulled the oxygen mask off, and said to Adrian Graves, "As I can feel excruciating pain in my legs, I doubt my back is broken. Get everyone safe, Celia knows what to do, all the last bits are on my desk. My wife is due at my digs by now. Tell her I love her."

Saul bore the stretcher journey down to the road with fortitude. At the police station, he was transferred to the yellow rescue helicopter and attended by the medics, while Royce was loaded in beside him. Adrian Graves and two other officers went with them to the hospital at Airedale. Adrian stayed with him while he was taken into casualty, and waited. He had never heard Saul Catchpole swear, but during the examination, he was made well aware that Saul had an extensive vocabulary. Before long, Saul was taken into theatre, and Adrian was met by a senior officer from Headquarters, who spoke to him about what had occurred, and then arranged for him to return to Settle, the roads being just passable.

Chapter Fifteen

Celia had the unpleasant job of explaining to Diana what had happened. Sam, white and quiet, was there, and listened. Diana was calm, but shaking, and asked, "Please, I would like to go to him. Can you get me there?"

"Yes, Mrs Catchpole, a traffic car is waiting to do so. Sam do you want to go as well?"

"No, I'll wait here, and go when he is feeling better, or get home and look after my sisters, if my aunt cannot. I must tell Chris and Lynn what the score is, and collect our things, and pay the bill there. Mum, can you help me out on that? Dad probably had his credit card on him. Is he going to die?"

"He is seriously injured, but from what I gather, he should make a full recovery, but I understand his leg was badly broken. They don't think his back was badly injured, but he does have serious injuries. Mo has kindly offered to look after you, Sam, and says you are welcome to stop with him, if you want to."

"Is Tatum all right? She was terribly upset about it, I know she ran back to help, but it was too late. If you don't mind, I'd like to see her and Brenda. I feel so helpless, but at least I can help them, if they want me to."

While Diana was whisked off to the hospital, the two remaining prisoners were booked in, and then interviewed. Greville decided to tell everything he knew, and sang like a canary, in the hopes of a lighter sentence, Windle maintained an obstinate silence, demanded a solicitor, and was taken to Skipton, to be detained there.

Diana was sitting by Saul's bedside when he came to, slowly and rather painfully. He was in a side room of his own, and a nurse was in attendance, having calmed Diana down, and provided her with tea and sympathy. She was reading a book, and didn't see him open his eyes.

"Darling, thanks for coming. Who is with the girls?"

"Ruth, but Sam said he would come back and take charge. Are you in a lot of pain?"

"A bit, I feel very woozy. Are you all right?"

"I will be, when you are. Can I get you anything?"

"No, I really want to sleep. I love you, very much, you know. I'm sorry I have been so distant recently. You wanted to tell me something, what was it?"

"That you were right about Ruth, and I am truly sorry. She is worse than ever. This happening has made me realise that you are the most important thing in my life. Forgive me?"

"Always. I wondered if you wanted me to move out. Just because I'm laid up, don't pretend, if that is what you want. I would rather know, even if I am going to be a cripple."

"No, Saul, I had already decided that you were right, and I was wrong, and then this happened. I love you, you rash, over-brave idiot. I knew the job had its risks, but there was no need to put yourself in danger. Don't ever do it again, do you hear?"

"No dear. Look, get home, love, and come and visit me when I'm a bit more sociable. Kick Ruth out, if you want to. I don't want her there when I get back, but if she can help you, then use her. You need to mend a few bridges with Sam and Stephen too, over her. I need to talk to the girls. I'm sorry, I'm going to sleep again. See you soon."

Diana spoke to the doctor before leaving the ward, and then was seen by the Assistant Chief Constable, who offered her a lift home, as he was not permitted a visit. Diana was very upset, and the ACC, who she knew quite well from social events, managed to get her to talk, and when he arrived at her home, she poured her heart out to him as they sat in the car outside. As Ruth came out to call them in, he said, "Will you be all right, do you want me to get her to go?"

"No, I have the strength now to deal with it. He is going to be all right, isn't he?"

"He will be off for some time, but yes, I believe so. It's early days yet. It leaves me in a jam, because I don't have anyone quite like him. Oh, I have other officers, all of them good at what they do, but he has his own way of doing things. I am sure that he will have recorded everything factual, but how he got there, we may have to talk to him to find out. Go on in, and my driver will call in about an hour for what you want to send him. What can we get him, to help his recovery?"

"If you really want to make him laugh, get him a video of 'Yes Minister', either that or 'Dad's Army'. I have already got him some books he would like, mainly Hardy, but there are others. As soon as he is allowed, a good single malt might help. He seldom drinks, but does enjoy one occasionally."

"Diana, promise me, if you need anything, ring me? I'll ring you in the morning, anyway, but I don't care what time it is, ring me?"

"Thanks, Mike, I will. You know, I always knew it could happen, every police wife does, but he was always so careful. At least he will recover, some widows are not so lucky."

"I know. This is part of my job I'm glad to do, but it is also one of the worst parts, when I have to deal with officers' families, left behind."

Diana went into the house. Ruth said very little, and occupied the girls while Diana packed.

The remainder of the family met in the dining room of the hotel, and Celia and several other officers were present. The family were told the basic facts of what had happened, and sat, stunned for a few minutes. In the pool room, the staff of the hotel were assembling for an emergency meeting. They were similarly told what had happened.

Celia announced, "Knowing what we do, I ask for your help, all of you. If there is anything else you can tell us, then we need to know it, now."

"Our mother is dead, and now you say my father killed her?"

"I'm afraid so, Miss Greywell. If he didn't actually strike the blow, then he helped. We have arranged for grief counsellors to attend here, if you want to use them, and you are free to return to your respective homes, if you want to. As soon as we can, the hotel will close for a week, get thoroughly cleaned, and then re-open. I have spoken to the staff, who are prepared to look after anyone who stays for a day or two. They have also very generously offered to withdraw the charge of theft against you, provided the money is returned."

"But I don't understand, why was Mum killed?"

"Because she saw something, and tried to blackmail the three of them about it, and they had to shut her up before she told the police about it."

"Officer, how is Superintendent Catchpole?" asked Ted Arbuthnot. "He was always civil, if a bit direct. I know he was always just doing his job."

"Not very well at all. He has had to have a lengthy operation, and may always have a limp. We have to wait and see."

"I'm sorry. He was nice to me, and my mother. Very fair. Now what do we do?"

"May I suggest that you talk to the solicitor, Mr Morrissey? He has offered to come in tomorrow morning and speak to all of you, about what happens now, Mr Arbuthnot."

"Yes, I'll certainly do that."

"But what I want to know," interrupted Wilfdred, "is how we can stop this Brenda woman getting all his money. Is she really our sister?"

"I believe so. I'm sure that she will be happy to provide DNA to prove it, but she is very shaken up."

"Wilfred, we have all of us got what we probably deserve," piped up Percy. Leave her alone. From what I saw of her she is rather pleasant. I think we either accept the situation or go our own way. I intend to offer the hand of friendship, anyway."

"You would, Percy. I hope she feels that she can give us some of the money, eventually. I think she should."

"If she has any sense, she will ignore the lot of us," said Alana. It's up to her. I will give her my number, maybe through the solicitor. If she wants to contact me, otherwise I intend to get on with my life. I never needed Uncle Cecil, nor did Ted. Mum has what she needs, and so do I. I fully intend to marry Miles, he asked me ages ago. Now I can. What are you going to do, Colin?"

"I don't know, Alana, look for another job I suppose. Move away, make a new start."

The family remained talking together, while Celia moved to the pool room where the staff of the hotel were assembling for an emergency meeting.

Celia called them to order, and said, "Mr Raistrick, we have already discussed where we go from here. I need to talk to several of the staff, and we will also need most of you as witnesses at any trial to follow. We need some further statements, especially about one or two things we have not covered already. Paul, did you identify your knife?"

"Yes, it was mine, but I don't think I want it back, thanks. I'll get another one. Is Brenda all right?"

"Not really, no, she is with her mother now, and her two brothers. Why?"

"We wondered if we could do anything."

"I leave that up to you, Giuseppe, will you tell us about that jewellery?"

"If I must. In my home town, in Italia, there was a saint, she came from a rich family, but went into holy orders. She gave her jewellery to the nuns, when she became one. It was very valuable, but it was a rich order, so it was kept there. Many year ago, it was stolen, and for many year, about two hundred, I think, the jewellery, she disappear. It was found eventually. But this a time, it had a curse on it, some story about the head nun, the Mother Superior, cursing the thieves. Every person who touch it have bads luck. Then it was returned to the Order, and once again, put on display.

"After the war, it was taken to the head of the Order, in Florence, for safety. I saw it, my mother she took me and my sister to see it when I was little boy. I went also with my brother, some year after. Then, it was stolen again. No one knew who take, but it had gone. There were big fuss about it, many papers print picture. It was thought jewel thief steal to sell in America. Our church, they pray often for it to return. Then I was in army, for short time, National Service. At the time the jewellery stolen, much work on bridge over river. British army there, to help, advice, with engineer.

"When I see Mrs Greywell with jewellery, I recognise it straight away. I thought maybe it was copy, but it look very good. I knew if it was real, then bad luck would come. I then understand why murder take place. I rang my sister in Italy that night, to ask about who to tell. Then, next morning, woman was dead. Where is jewellery now?"

"We have found it in Mr Windle's room. If as you say, it is stolen, then in time it will be returned to its rightful owners. I will need to speak to you about that, thank you. Wendy we need to talk to you, as well."

"You want to know if I knew it was Greywell who caused my father to become bankrupt, all those years ago? Yes, I knew, but it was a long time ago, and I spoke to my mother about it. She and I feel that Dad rather brought it on himself. I had no liking for Greywell, but I decided to put all that behind me long ago."

"We will be here for at least a couple of days, and we need to sort a lot of things out, especially with you, Mr Raistrick. All you staff have been wonderful to us, helped us in every way. Thank you so much. We have quite a bit of clearing up to do, but my governor will be thanking you properly, when he gets here. He is taking over from Superintendent Catchpole."

In the custody suite at Skipton, Greville was still talking, and Windle was stalwartly maintaining his silence. At the hospital, Royce was being carefully guarded. His guards told him nothing, and watched his every move. In another ward, Saul was sleeping, restlessly, and woke in some pain, before he was given some pain relief by a concerned doctor. It soon took effect, and the doctor, a pleasant young man said, "Is there anything else I can do for you? Anyone you want to see tomorrow?"

"I need to talk to my Detective Inspector. Explain a few things I didn't have time to write down. I hate being laid up, how long must I stay in here?"

"A while, I'm afraid. You could have died, you know. It will take time to get you back on your feet. Thankfully, your back is uninjured, but the bruising will take a while to come out. Yes, you will walk again, but it will take time, and rest. That is what you need at the moment, rest, plenty of it. The sooner you stop fretting, the quicker you will mend."

"In other words, stop being a bad patient, and accept the inevitable. I'll be good, I promise, but there are things I need to explain, and do. Then I can relax."

"Then I will ring your headquarters and speak to the policeman who was here earlier. Do you want a radio or television?"

"Later, yes. Now I just feel very sick, and my head aches."

"If you will try flying into cliffs, it will. The painkillers should ease it. Try to get some more sleep. That will help."

"I feel like I have been asleep for days, already."

"You have, for two days almost. I'll call the nurse in, she can freshen you up, then you can have books or TV if you want."

It was not much later that Saul drifted off to sleep again, this time an easier sleep. While he slept, Royce was moved to custody, and was charged, and then remanded to a prison hospital, while Greville and Windle were remanded in custody, having been charged.

Chapter Sixteen

Saul came to, feeling much easier and more refreshed, three days later. He was, for the first time, hungry and very thirsty. He took notice of the room around him, and was surprised to see flowers and a host of cards in the room. He had never socialised much with his work colleagues, and suspected that many of the cards were from his family and social friends, fellow walkers and artists. He remembered Diana being with him several times, but each time it had seemed like a dream.

Feeling more himself, he tried to sit up, and was hampered by a plastercast on his arm, and his leg was in traction. His efforts soon made him stop, his ribs hurt sharply. By the bed was a buzzer, in reach of his good hand. Even that hand had dressings on it. He felt hot and clammy. He contemplated ringing the buzzer, but decided his needs were not an emergency. Soon, a nurse came in, a young man.

"Hello, you are awake. Feeling better?"

"That is relative. Yes, I suppose so. I'm really sticky, and thirsty. Can I have something to drink?"

"Yes, of course, do you want juice, tea, water, or something else?"

With a wry smile, Saul said, "I suppose a whisky and soda is out of the question? Yes, I thought so, in which case, I'll opt for a cup of tea, or coffee."

"Tea it is then. Do you feel up to any visitors yet? There is a list as long as my arm of people wanting to see you. Your wife is due in this afternoon, but your colleagues are waiting very patiently until the doctor thinks you are up to it."

"I don't want to see anyone until I have had a wash and a shave, and eaten a decent meal. What day is it?"

"It is the twenty-third of December. Thursday, and it is half past seven in the morning."

"Then I have been out some time."

"Yes, you have been pretty ill, very feverish, not surprising considering all the bruising you had. It can give you a fever. Then of course, you were allergic to the antibiotics. That didn't help."

"I had no idea, which ones? I've never had a problem before, but I haven't been ill in a long time."

Washed, shaved and feeling much better, Saul sat up in the bed, and looked at the meal in front of him, on its tray. It looked insipid, and when he tried some, it tasted of nothing. Hunger prompted him to finish it. The nurse returned, and said, "Did you enjoy it?"

"No, it tasted of cotton wool. Can't I have a proper meal? I'm still hungry."

"Later, you are on the mend! You have a visitor, two, in fact. Shall I show them in?"

"Who?"

"An Assistant Chief Constable, and a Detective Inspector, a woman."

"Yes, do."

Celia was shocked when she saw Saul. He looked almost skinny and very pale, and his face had lines, and his eyes looked pained and tired. He managed a smile, and said, "How is it going?"

"All under control, except for a few ends to tie up. Royce tried to top himself in custody, but failed, because he was being watched. When he saw he was not going to be able to, he started to talk, and is spilling everything, which coincides with what Greville says. Windle will say nothing. I have dozens of messages for you, from everyone on the team, and at The Golden Lion. Also the Coroner, and Mr Morrissey, who wants to see you sometime soon, and so does young Tatum, and Mo. Your son has been in several times to see you, but you were very ill, so he said he would come back. Your elder son came to see me, and asked what had happened. He said, if I saw you, that the problem of Ruth was solved, and not to worry about it. Saul, we need your statement rather soon. Shall I send in a stenographer, and tell me what to bring in, and I will get it done today?"

"Stephen, here? Oh, good. Yes, Celia, please do. Can you please arrange for young Tatum to come and see me? I need to talk to her."

"Has she done something wrong?"

"Quite the opposite, but I doubt she feels that way. No, she did exactly what I told her to, an admirable quality, I want to tell her that. She was very brave, you know. Sir, I want her and Mo commended. Thanks for coming, Mike, you can cut all the usual welfare speech, I know it by heart!"

Celia blushed, but looked at Saul, and saw him wink at her. His eyes suddenly seemed very alive. Mike laughed and said, "Now I know you are on the mend, I want to tell you that as soon as you have done what you have to, to tie this case up, you are going away with your wife to convalesce. There is a place at the nursing home at Goring, if you want it, but you decide. We have brought some things in to cheer you up. I have acquired a TV and video, and some things you might enjoy. We managed to find all the 'Yes Minister' tapes, and a few others besides. Here is a mobile phone, and I have put any numbers you may need on it. You are stuck in here until well after New Year, so use it, if you want to. Royce has been charged with your attempted murder, and that of his stepdaughter. The chocolates he sent her were heavily laced with Rohypnol, and he intended to push her off the cliff. The others were standing by to help if necessary. They had a story all ready, and he was going into her house to remove the chocolates and note, once they had checked she was dead. Listen, Saul, we need you, back at work as soon as we can. You are under orders to be a perfect patient, and get well without delay. All the things we have turned up in this case are the basis for a large fraud investigation."

"I hate fraud cases!"

"I know, which is why it has gone to the Fraud Squad, but if you don't get better as soon as is possible, you might yet end up on the squad!"

"I suppose my promotion's gone west."

"Not at all. I had a chat with your surgeon. It seems you should make a reasonable recovery. So long as you promise not to wrestle with suspects on cliff tops again, I see no reason why the whole of CID shouldn't be yours on your return. I need to talk to you about what happened."

"I know, it's all right, Celia can stay. I misjudged the situation. I had no idea how close to cracking, or desperation, he was. I didn't expect him to rush me like that. I should have taken its possibility into account. I didn't."

"Which is so unlike you, that I wonder what you were thinking of."

"I had something else, personal, on my mind. It distracted me. The last thing I expected was for him to pull me off with him. What are his injuries?"

"Broken ankle, and two broken fingers, cuts and bruises. You cushioned his fall. What you did was still brave."

"I don't think so, foolish more like. You see, Celia, we all make mistakes, let other things distract us, me included. I can't actually remember any you have made, but since my bang on the head, quite a few things seem to have slipped my memory."

Once again, she saw his piercing stare, and a twinkle in his eye as he looked away. She saw a slight smile on his lips. She looked away, and felt a flood of relief when she understood he was forgiving her.

"I'm missing something here. You two obviously have something else in mind. If you ever forgot anything in your life, Saul, then it is the first I have heard of it. Whatever happened, I don't want to know."

"Wise decision, Mike. Some things are best kept within the confines of a team. Now, can I read their confessions?"

"Not today, no. We need your statement first. Then I would like your comments on them. I'll be in to see you soon."

Mike left, and Celia got up to go, but Saul held her sleeve. When the door had shut, she turned to him, and said, "Thank you."

"No need. I know it won't ever happen again. If it does, I shall recover my memory, fair?"

"Very. Do you want me to come and see you again?"

"Yes, how else can I find out what is going on? You must tell me everything, and then I shall need the usual, grapes, whiskey, chocolates, flowers, night gown, candle, crutches, silly hat and…"

"And I'm not that much of a fool. Sir, of course I'll tell you, if I don't the rest of the team will be doing it at dead of night. They might bring you whiskey, and a load of things that you shouldn't have. They will anyway, I expect."

"Yes, I was wondering how soon one of the lads would turn up in drag, as a nurse. When we are on our own, Celia, I would rather you called me Saul. What are you doing over Christmas?"

"Nothing, Working I expect."

"If you are bored, and want to humour an old man, come and see me. I know you play cards, so do I."

"Thanks, Saul, I will."

As she got up to go, Diana walked in.

"Hello, Celia, they said you were here. I'm so glad you came, he won't fret so much now. Thank you for what you did for me and Sam the other day. I know you well enough to trust you won't overtire him, but stop him from getting bored."

"He seems to be better. I need to settle up with you, for lodgings and that, most of which the Force will pay for. I'll wait for you downstairs."

Diana sat on the chair beside the bed. Saul looked at her.

"You look almost your normal self. You were very ill, darling. We were worried about you. Stephen came back."

205

"So I understand, and I hear he sorted Ruth out. How?"

"I'll tell you another time."

"Please tell me now. It might make me cheer up."

"Saul, he was wonderful. Our little boy has become a fine man. He asked her why she needed to criticize and snipe at you all the time, and why she was intent on breaking you and me up. When she said she thought I was better than that, and you were holding me back from my true destiny, he calmly said that she was no longer welcome in your house, and he would assist her packing. He said that whatever her personal disappointments were, she would no longer hold any sway in his father's house, and offered to drive her home. They had a massive row, and in the end, he went up to the spare room, threw her things in a case, put them in the mini, and almost carried her out of the house. He told her if she ever upset me like that again, he would be round to sort her out, and mentioned that while you were incapacitated, as the eldest son, he was merely deputising for you."

"Poor Diana. Are you very upset?"

"No, I'm not, I'm very relieved. I feel free at last. I do love you, you know that?"

"Yes, I know. When you rang and said you needed to talk to me, I thought you were going to tell me you wanted to leave me."

"I thought as much. That is why you misread that man? I'm sorry."

"No, I should have trusted you. Have you a spare place at the Christmas Dinner table?"

"Yes, but you can't come home that soon."

"No silly, could you invite Celia? She is on her own. She needs a friend or two just at the moment."

"Fine, but Sam has also invited two friends, one a girlfriend he seems to have acquired, called Tatum, and the other is a man called Moriarty. Is he taking the Mick?"

"No, and I'm glad. I like Mo, and so will you. If any of you get the chance, come and see me."

Saul made his statement, and by the time he had finished, he was exhausted, and was left to sleep the night through. The next day, after his breakfast, Tatum knocked on the door, and came in.

"Tate, I'm so glad you came. I want to thank you so much for what you did."

"But you got hurt, and it was my fault, I should have stopped and helped you, not run away."

"No. You did exactly as I ordered you to, and expected. Had you got involved, then not only might I be injured, but I would have had your injury and death on my conscience as well. I am so proud of you, and the help you gave me and the rest of the team. I needed to explain that to you, that I am well pleased with you. I am grateful that you didn't complicate matters. Thank you for helping young Brenda, too."

"How did you know I'd been to see her?"

"I didn't, but I thought you would. Is my son behaving himself with you?"

"Yes, as much as I want him to. He invited me over for Christmas Day. Do you mind?"

"No. I approve. Now, is he here?"

"Yes, but you had said you wished to see me. I'll leave you two to talk. Thank you for telling me that. It makes me feel much better. Oh, DI Allenby sent these papers for you, said something about interesting bedtime reading. Bye!"

Chapter Seventeen

Saul finished his tea, and then took up the papers, and opened the first envelope. He managed to find his reading glasses, and put them on. He made himself as comfortable as he could, and turned to the first page:

'I make this statement of my own free will. I have been told that I need not say anything, and that whatever I say may be given in evidence. This statement is true. TR Royce

I was born in Wiltshire, in Salisbury. My mother was a teacher, and my father, also a teacher, died when I was small. My mother was a religious woman, and I was an only child. I went to the grammar school, and then on to university, where I studied Dentistry. In the last year of my course, my mother died of a heart attack. We were never rich, and money was always a struggle. I joined the Army Dentistry Corps, but I hated it. It was not long before I hit serious money problems, and needed to find a way out. I did some work as a locum, when I left the army, and it was while I was working in Peckham that I met Greville Greywell. He made me proposition, about a scam to move jewels round the world. I used to hide gems in teeth, and dentures for him, fit them to his runners, and remove them if required. He never said, but I knew that most of them were either stolen or smuggled. It was through him that I met his brother, Cecil Greywell. I later found out that Cecil was the brains behind the whole thing. I was doing quite well for a time, but then we nearly got caught. One of the couriers died, and a post mortem examination revealed the hidden diamonds in his teeth. I had to get out of the area in a hurry. I appealed to Greville and Cecil for help. It was Cecil who came up with an escape for me. He had got a girl into trouble, at least that is how he described it, and he said if I married the girl, and looked after the child, then he would set me up as a dentist in Yorkshire. He made the offer look very attractive. It was even better when I met the woman, Doreen Williams, and found her attractive. I am, in fact, very fond of her. I wasn't faithful, but I tried my best. For this service, Cecil Greywell paid me, every so often, either in money, or more often in land. It was from him I got the two farms. He didn't want to deal directly with me, so it was all done through Oliver Windle. I still had to do the occasional gem dental work, but that was usually at Greville's request. For many years I have had a gambling problem, so I always needed money. My whole life has been a gamble. Before I married Doreen, Cecil had already settled some money on her, but he couldn't leave it alone. He wanted to know about the child, Brenda. I used to provide him with reports and some photographs, always through Windle. I have always been rather good at being a dentist, but it never provided me with enough money, not for my wants. I had to pretend to be a country dentist, and a family man. Doreen wanted more children, and Oliver said that in order to keep her happy, Cecil had promised to look after them, so we had the two boys. It wasn't long after the youngest was born that Doreen found out that I was gambling. I had to hide it from her much more carefully. She became much more suspicious, and our romance, such as it was, faded. She seemed happy with her lot, and with her children. As soon as Brenda left school, I decided to talk Doreen into making her independent, but Brenda is a bright girl, and I had to be careful. I put the house we bought her into my name, because I wanted to be able to control her. I didn't want her to ever find out what was going on. I had been assured that Cecil would never acknowledge Brenda, and that I would get some money to allow for my retirement. This would come to me from Oliver. I had a bad fright when Brenda fell for a lad called Nathan. I sensed that I could lose control over that, so I bought the lad off, and sent him down south. I had another fright when Brenda announced that she wished to become a police officer, not something I wanted. Brenda was always a trusting child, and I was finding it more and more difficult to manipulate her. Then Doreen found out about one of my affairs. Once again, I approached Windle, and explained that things were dodgy, and he said he would see what he could do. Cecil always had a team of men around him, who were either from his army days, or bound to him in some way. I knew that some of them would stop at nothing. I was not involved, but I am pretty certain that Cecil had at least two enemies of his knocked off. Oliver knows, I think. Then the unexpected happened. Cecil sent a message that he wanted to see Brenda. It was just after he had a minor heart attack, and he lost the plot, completely. All his promises were discarded. I could see that there was serious trouble ahead. My only hope was to accumulate as much money as I could, and do a bunk, abroad somewhere. I needed the money I had been promised, and I needed to leave enough to keep Doreen and the boys, so they could believe that I was dead, and wouldn't start too deep an investigation. Cecil announced his intended visit to Settle. I knew why, and so did Oliver. I had to be very careful. This was my turf, and I was known here, and could be recognised. They arrived, and Brenda soon worked out that she was in some way related to Cecil. The family had a meeting, and Oliver told me what had happened at it. He mentioned that Jim, the brother-in-law, knew something very dangerous to all of us. Cecil discussed with Oliver what to do about it. They decided that the safest thing to do was to kill Jim, but things went a bit wrong. Jim was fit, and an unarmed combat expert. Oliver and Cecil got his man, Charlie, to call Jim late one night, and they got him up by the bathroom, near Cecil's room. There was a hell of a fight, Oliver held the man from behind, and Charlie knifed him, but got a bit knocked about. They cleaned the worst of the mess up in the bathroom, and the two of them dragged the body downstairs in a sheet they took from the linen cupboard. They were going to take it outside, but there was a policeman patrolling outside, and they put it in the settle as a temporary measure. Cecil came to see me, and passed me a message while he was at my surgery, to call and see him. My wife sometimes helps out at functions at the Golden Lion, and still had a back door key, which I took, and the next night I let myself in when everyone had gone to bed, and Charlie, Oliver and Cecil met in room five, to discuss it. They wanted me to get rid of the body in my Land Rover, somewhere on one of the farms. I explained it would be difficult, very hard, because the ground was as hard as iron, and the tattoos on Jim's body were very distinctive. Then Greville walked in on us, and said he knew what had happened. He suggested that he meet me in his car, and transfer the body to my Land Rover, away from Settle, and we dump the body miles away, and put it in water somewhere. Charlie said he would have to get away, as it wouldn't be long before someone connected him forensically with the body, once it was found. He demanded a massive sum from Cecil to keep his mouth shut and disappear. When Cecil agreed, I knew that he would never pay it. Oliver grabbed hold of him, and Cecil took up a scalpel that he already had in a drawer, that he must have taken from my surgery, and stabbed him. We carried his body downstairs, but it wouldn't fit in the settle, and then we heard someone moving around, and the only place to hide him in a hurry was the telephone cupboard. It took me and Oliver ages to push him into the hole, and then we knew we would never get him out. We washed up, and I took our clothes home with me when I left, and burnt them in my

211

incinerator the next day. Oliver got rid of the scalpel later. Then Cecil dropped his bombshell. He told me that he was going to leave most of his money to Brenda, who he was preparing to acknowledge. Oliver and I got very worried. He was no longer trustworthy. We met up in Watery Lane, and talked about it. Oliver said we would have to involve Greville, but I didn't want to. Then he told me that he had found out that Cecil had written everything, about all of us, and it was in his house at York. If that got into the wrong hands, then we were all finished. Oliver had pinched Cecil's keys, which he gave to me, and I took impressions of them, and sat up half the night, making duplicates. The night of the snow, that Cecil died, I had a busy night. During the evening, I went over to York, and got into his house, and found the documents. I looked through them, and took out everything that was dangerous to all of us. I searched for duplicates, but couldn't find any. I rang Greville when I set off back, on the phone in the cupboard in the pub. I told him to meet me at Hellifield, so I could tell him what the score was. The storm was a hindrance, and the stupid man was so pissed, he put his car into a snow drift, and couldn't get it out. We were talking about what to do, when this quarry lorry turned up, and I pretended I was just a passer-by, and Greville got a lift back with him, and I went home, and as soon as Doreen was asleep, I snuck back into the pub with my key. The three of us, Oliver, Greville and me found Cecil in the Writing room, and Greville and I held him, while Oliver cut his throat. There was no way we could hide that, so I told the other two to shower, and then we put the lights out, and I watched as several passers-by walked down the road. It was snowing something dreadful. That policeman Graves was on patrol. I saw him talking to someone, and waited while he walked off, and got home as soon as I could. I had told the other two to get rid of the knife, and their clothes. Before I left, Oliver had found the file with those damn photos in, of Brenda, and I took them to the safe in the surgery, until I could burn them. I expect you have found them by now. All that evening I had worn surgical gloves. I gave the others some too. Oliver told me that Ruby had been saying she had seen Greville and him, and me, coming out of the Writing Room that night. She wanted money to keep her mouth shut. Greville wanted her out of the way, anyway. She was getting very troublesome. Oliver spiked her drink, once he knew, and after everyone had gone to bed, she was sitting alone in the bar. He told me that she never even felt it when he killed her, and he picked her up, and put her in the freezer. It was stupid, but there was an officer on patrol outside, and he didn't dare move her further afield. I began to panic. I needed to be sure I would get enough to do a bunk. Then I spoke to Brenda, and she asked me if I had been out that night. I had no idea she had seen me. I denied it, and when I went to see her at her house later, after Ruby had been killed, I knew she suspected me. I couldn't afford that. I knew that sooner or later, I would have to get rid of her. I told her it would be a good idea to make a will. I even checked she had. I met the other two, and explained the danger. They wanted her out of the way, and we agreed to share what I got. You hadn't even interviewed me, and I thought I was in the clear. We had to act fast. The best thing was an accident, and I sent her some chocolates. They were drugged, so she would be dopey, and I rang her. I realise now, that Catchpole was on to us, and outwitted us. I thought we could get away with it. I knew that Lewis had given her some sleeping tablets; I saw them when I called, so I used the same thing, and rang her, asking her to meet me, up on Castleberg. What I hadn't bargained for was the decoy. Until she was really close, I thought it was Brenda. Then I was trapped. Everything was ruined. I knew it was Catchpole, even though we had never actually met, I had seen him over the previous few days. He knew everything. He had to. I hated him, and hoped, if I took him with me, not all of it would come out. He tried to arrest me, but he is not a heavy man, and I thought he wouldn't hold me, but he did. He is stronger than he looked. I hoped I could either be killed, or if I was lucky, get away, He wouldn't let go. I hated him, and decided to take him with me. I landed on him, and he was obviously badly injured, but the bastard still wouldn't let go. Then you lot got to us, and I realised I had failed. You asked me what was in the syringe, it was more of the sleeping drug. I have nothing more to lose now, and no hope of anything, so I have decided to tell you everything. My main regret is that my sons will have the shame of this hanging over them. Doreen got what she wanted, and as for Brenda, it was always just a commercial arrangement. It was difficult pretending to be in a loving relationship, with another man's child to bring up. She is a nice kid, but not mine. Doreen can divorce me now, and I'm sure Brenda will look after her, and the boys. She is a lot more clever than I thought. If I can escape the consequences of what I did, I will, but I never want to see any of my family again. I wish I could say that I was sorry, but I'm not. I gambled, for high stakes, and lost. I accept that I will never see freedom again. I can say nothing in mitigation. I will write to Doreen, and explain. I doubt she will forgive me. TR Royce.'

Saul lay thinking for some time. He turned to another statement, and read it; Greville was not as ordered or as literate in his confession. He confirmed almost everything that Royce had said, but in the final page, Saul read:

'My wife, Ruby, was always a dangerous woman. In her younger days she was clever, and very tight lipped. As she became more alcoholic, she couldn't keep her mouth shut, and when she told me she had seen something, I told her to shut up about it, like I told the policeman, but she stupid woman tried to put the squeeze on Oliver, and he finished her off. I couldn't bring myself to do so, I'm squeamish about killing women, but he isn't. Oliver has been with Cecil for many years. He learned a lot about how to kill people when he was younger. At one time he worked as a mortuary attendant, before he had some legal training. I didn't want to kill young Brenda either, but I saw the need to do it, I agreed to help Royce with it, so did Oliver. It was Cecil who taught me to be ruthless. He was my elder brother. When we were children there were three of us boys. Our other brother was called Neville, and he was always sneaking around, and telling tales. He had an unfortunate accident when he was thirteen. He drowned, when he and Cecil were out boating on a lake. Cecil said he tried to save him, but I saw. It was Cecil what drowned him. I was frightened of Cecil from that day on, I knew what he was capable of. It was after that, when our parents adopted Julia. Mama was that upset at losing her favourite darling spoiled brat, she needed another child. Neville always got the best. She spoiled him. I hated him too. I think our father always suspected Cecil, and me. I hated him, so did Cecil. Papa was a bully, I never heard him say a kind word to either of us.'

Saul knew that most of his case was solved, and he lay thinking about it. The nurse found him fast asleep, still clutching the papers, an hour later. She put them in an envelope, and carefully took his reading glasses off his face, and dimmed the light.

At her home, Diana sat, preparing vegetables for the Christmas dinner. Stephen and Sam were helping her, and the two girls were watching the television in the next room. Diana felt relaxed, and said, "Do you forgive me, boys?"

"Yes, Mum, we do. Sam and I have been talking. We don't want Ruth here again, because she is like a black shadow over the house. We know why she hates Dad, but what did we ever do? No, Mum, it is time we became a proper family again. We think you have made the right choice. Dad would never have made you choose, but his nearly dying has. Sam and I have decided that we are going to take the girls over to the Isle of

Man, for a couple of weeks when he comes out of hospital, so you can have some time together. Would you like a drink, Mum? I would, and I know just where Dad keeps the whiskey."

Doreen Royce sat with her two sons and Brenda in her lounge. They had almost done crying, and were sitting shell shocked, wondering what to do next. Doreen said, "I should be sorting something out for dinner tomorrow, but I don't feel like it. Could we leave it a few days?"

"I asked at the pub, they will let us have a Christmas dinner there, Mum. Hell, who is that at he door?"

Elaine and her husband came in, and Elaine said, "Look, we wondered, once I have finished at the pub, would you all come round to our place, for quiet meal? Nothing special, but we thought you might not feel like celebrating. The boys can bring their presents. Wendy is going to be there too. You would be most welcome."

"God bless you, Elaine, yes, we will. Thank you. You always were a good friend. Life will change for us, won't it? What are we going to do?"

"Don't worry, Mum," Brenda said. "I will look after you and the boys, and when you are right, I'm going to join the police force. I've decided. I do hope that poor Mr Catchpole is better. He protected me, you know. He really cared that I was safe. Now I can hope to do the same for other people. We will survive. We know who cares about us. Mo was round earlier, and Tate, not to mention lots of our friends. We are still alive, and we have the rest of our lives to be grateful for it. Come on, let's have a drink. There are carol singers outside. I love you all, thank you."

Chapter Eighteen

Chief Superintendent Catchpole had given his evidence, and walked slowly out of the witness box. He still needed to use a stick, and his slight limp was a nuisance, but it would lessen in time. He had not long returned to duty. His convalescence had been slow and he had taken up swimming, to strengthen his weak leg. He left the court and moved slowly over to the canteen, where he found Tatum, Sam and Brenda sitting at a table. Sam jumped up and bought him a coffee, and as Saul sat down, Sam said, "How did it go?"

"Much as I expected, thanks, Sam. Well done, Tatum, I understand you gave your evidence well, as did you, Brenda. Now we just have to wait for the verdict on Windle. I know what Tatum and Sam have planned, what are you going to do now, Brenda?"

"I have taken the advice of Mr Morrissey. I have set up a trust fund for the boys, and my mother, and when it all comes through they should be well looked after. Personally, I have decided to get on with my life. Wilfred wanted me to give him money, but I won't. I have sent in my application to join the police. Dr Lewis said he would give me a reference, and so did Patrick. My stepfather signed over the house to me, and I've sold it, and bought another one. My mother says she has got over it, and she seems much happier now. How arc you? I never really

217

got a chance to thank you properly. Are you going to stay in the police?"

"Yes, for a while at least. Soon I hope to start walking again, something I always enjoyed. I wish you luck in the force. Now Tatum and Sam seem to be an item, my wife and I have more time together, and the girls are doing well at their new school. I spoke to Patrick the other day. This whole business set the hotel back, but business is picking up now, and he tells me that he is going to miss you dreadfully when you move on. At the moment, I understand that the press seem to be staying there, en masse. Which reminds me, they are outside in numbers. If you wish to avoid them, we can get you out the back way. They are baying for a statement as soon as the case finishes. I have been told I must give it to them."

"Yes, I wanted to ask you about that. I have avoided them so far, but I do want to say something to them, when this is over. I have written down what I want to say. Mr Morrissey is here, he says he will read it to them. He said I should show it to you, so you know what to expect. Have they given you a hard time?"

"They have tried, yes. One in particular, that man Andrews, tried to make a big thing of my getting injured. He's out there now, and I shall have difficulty being civil to him. He laid siege to the hospital while I was there, and I got thoroughly fed up with it. If that is what you want to say, then I have no objection, but thank you, it is nice to know we can get some things right. How are you lot getting back to Settle?"

"Mr Morrissey is taking me back. Me and a friend, who came to support me. Here they are now. "

Saul looked up, and smiled at Morrissey, and got up and shook his hand. He looked at the young man with the solicitor.

"Paul isn't it? I remember you, you are the chef at the Golden Lion, I think? I see. You are here to support Brenda for today?"

"Not just for today, if I have my way. I plan to be around her for some time if she will let me. Can I get anyone another coffee, or something to eat? They have some decent chocolate cake on sale?"

Paul and Sam went off and brought back a tray of drinks and cakes. Saul moved over as two more chairs were pulled up.

"Would you like some chocolate cake, Brenda?"

"No thanks, I've sort of gone off chocolate recently. I decided to change my name after this is over. Mum has too, and both the boys asked to. We are going back to Williams. Are you not having any cake?"

"No. After all the rest I've had to take, I need to watch my weight. I started to put it on when I was laid up. It has taken ages to get it off. I never did like sweet stuff much. So tell me young lady, is this serious between you and Paul?"

"Yes, I think it is. I have had a lot of attention from men since I inherited money, and I saw it for what it was. Paul hasn't changed one bit. I always did like him, and it turns out he liked me, so we will just have to see how things go. Did you know Patrick is putting the pub up for sale?"

"Yes, he said. Why?"

"Well Paul has decided that he wants to move on, so he is looking for another job. We will wait and see where I am posted. You know who wants to buy it?"

"Not you?"

"No way, but Mo does. He would be very good as a boss, I think. He would be an excellent landlord. Straight as a die. He has been a great friend, helped us out a lot."

Saul spoke to Morrissey later. They decided what to say at the press conference, and then Morrissey said, "I heard you talking to young Brenda. I approve of Paul, and I have set things up so she will be protected, with all that money. She insists on quite a large donation to Police charities. Incidentally, I rather fancy that Mo and Doreen might be taking the pub on together. There is more to Mo's helpfulness than just a feeling of duty. Doreen has certainly encouraged it. Brenda asked me to make sure that the money was available to her mother, should she want to use it for that. I know you will be a welcome guest there, if you ever want a holiday."

"I might just do that. Now we wait until the jury comes in. If you will excuse me, I must go and find the rest of my team."

"I last saw them heading into the reading room behind the barristers' library. I know the seats are more comfortable in there. I'll catch up with you later."

Saul sighed with relief when the verdict came back as guilty. He waited while sentence was passed, and then went out to face the press. In the front of the pack was Andrews, who was pushing and vying with others to ask questions. Amongst the pack was a face he knew, and was surprised to see. When Saul had given his statement, and Morrissey had read out his, Saul saw Andrews trip over, and scrabble on the ground. Saul watched in surprise as his son, Stephen, melted into the crowd, with a rather smug grin on his face. Saul made a quick getaway.

Later that evening, when he was home and sitting in the armchair, Diana beside him, Sam came in with Stephen.

"Well done, Dad, another successful case! I have news for you. I have got a transfer with my firm over this way. Sam says you might know of a flat to rent, in town. How about it?"

"For both of you, to share? Seems a sound idea. Incidentally, I have a bone to pick with you, Stephen. Since when do you mix with the press?"

"I couldn't resist it, after the way he hounded you. He was that intent on giving you a hard time, that he fell over his own feet. How do you cope with low life like that?"

"Not easily. Are you two off to bed?"

"No way, we are off out, clubbing. We will try not to wake you when we come in. Who the hell is ringing you this time of night?"

Saul picked up the phone beside his chair,

"Saul Catchpole. Where? Who is there? Then call DI Allenby, and tell her I will be there in an hour. Call the team in. I'm on my way."

"Oh, no, Saul, not another case?"

"I'm afraid so, darling, it is what I do. I'll ring you when I can."

"I know. You needn't look so happy at the idea. Take care!"

Diana watched with amusement while Saul sprang up, with vitality in his step. He left the house with an overnight bag, and drove off into the night. His listlessness had gone, and he was once again in harness. She knew he had made a full recovery. She put the kettle on.